What's her problem?

Jessica scowled. "I want my shirt back. Now," she said with a stubborn glint in her blue-green eyes.

"Are you kidding?" I stared at her, feeling a twinge of annoyance. Angry or not, she was acting like a total freak. "It's the middle of the day!"

Jessica didn't answer. She just tapped her foot impatiently and stared pointedly at the shirt.

"You're the one who walked into my room last week and flung the shirt at me, like I was from some kind of used-clothes garbage dump," I said hotly. "You were the one who said I had to take it because it was poisoning the other clothes in your closet with its uncoolness."

"Whatever." Jessica spun on her heel and stomped off into the cafeteria.

"What's wrong with *her*?" Anna said, staring after my sister in astonishment.

"Yeah," Salvador commented. "It's like she had a personality transplant or something." He shrugged. "Not that she was perfect before. It's like Mr. Hyde and Mr. Hydier."

I glared after her, still steaming over her idiotic tantrum. "I have no idea what's going on with her," I told my friends. "But she'd better get over it soon."

Don't miss any of the books in SWEET VALLEY JUNIOR HIGH, an exciting series from Bantam Books!

I'm So Outta Here

Written by
Jamie Suzanne

Created by
FRANCINE PASCAL

BANTAM BOOKS
NEW YORK • TORONTO • LONDON • SYDNEY • AUCKLAND

RL 4, 008-012

I'M SO OUTTA HERE
A Bantam Book / September 2000

Sweet Valley Junior High is a trademark of Francine Pascal.
Conceived by Francine Pascal.
Cover photography by Michael Segal.

Produced by 17th Street Productions,
an Alloy Online, Inc. company.
33 West 17th Street
New York, NY 10011.

ISBN: 0-553-48723-X

Visit us on the Web! www.randomhouse.com/kids

Published simultaneously in the United States and Canada

Bantam Books is an imprint of Random House Children's Books, a
division of Random House, Inc. BANTAM BOOKS and the rooster
colophon are registered trademarks of Random House, Inc. Bantam Books,
1540 Broadway, New York, New York 10036.

PRINTED IN THE UNITED STATES OF AMERICA

OPM   0 9 8 7 6 5 4 3 2 1

To Anders Johansson

Jessica

"Oh! I almost forgot," my mom said as she pulled a dish of lasagna out of the oven. "I finally heard back from the housepainters. They can start Friday morning."

I stared hungrily at the dish in her hands. "That's great, Mom," I said, a little distracted by my growling stomach. I'd had track practice that afternoon, and I was starving. I knew my parents were excited about the renovations they were doing on our house, but personally, I didn't find it all that thrilling. I mean, it was cool that they'd decided to have my room painted and Elizabeth's too, but it wasn't like they were installing water beds or anything.

"So"—Mom pushed aside a few strands of blond hair as she took her place at the table and looked back and forth between me and Elizabeth—"you girls are probably going to have to move into the den for a week."

I looked across the table at Elizabeth, who was picking at her salad. So we were going to be roomies, huh? Now, that could actually be pretty cool. Don't get me wrong—I wasn't looking forward to being kicked out of my room for a week, but a week in the den with Elizabeth sounded like it might be fun. I couldn't remember the last time my twin and I had had a good old-fashioned slumber party—just the two of us. I was sure it had been back before our school was rezoned to Sweet Valley Junior High at the beginning of the year. Since then we'd both been way too busy making new friends, finding our way around, and basically getting used to a whole new place. It would be nice to hang out with each other for a week, sleeping in the den, catching up and talking after lights-out the way we used to.

I was sure Elizabeth would be thinking the same thing. That happens a lot when you're twins—you read each other's minds. I kicked Elizabeth under the table, and when she looked up, I grinned at her conspiratorially. This was going to be great! Elizabeth smiled back at me—she looked excited too. It was obvious we were on the same wavelength.

Elizabeth wiped her mouth with a napkin and rested both elbows on the table. "Um, do you think I could spend the week at Anna's?" she asked, looking first at my dad, then my mom, and tugging on her long, blond ponytail nervously.

I felt my smile sag, then disappear. Apparently, Liz and I had been grinning about two completely different things. She wanted to spend the whole week with Anna? That wasn't exactly what I was expecting her to say. What had happened to our twin wavelength?

My parents looked a little surprised too. "You want to stay with Anna for a whole week?" Mom exchanged a doubtful look with Dad.

"Well, they have tons of room, and it would be much more comfortable than squeezing onto the couch with Jessica. And Anna and I could get tons of work done on *Zone*," Elizabeth replied eagerly.

I held my breath. Mom and Dad were going to say no—they *had* to say no. They would realize that spending that much time writing articles and stuff would be bad for Elizabeth's health. And Anna was nice and all, but I was sure she could get really boring after a while. Did Elizabeth even know what she was getting herself into?

"I'm worried you'd be imposing on Mr. and Mrs. Wang, Liz," my dad said.

"Don't worry," Elizabeth said earnestly. "Anna just told me her dad is going out of town for a business trip. So it would just be Anna and her mom. And me, of course." She smiled. "Besides," she added, looking more and more confident by the second, "if they don't want me to stay over, they can always say no."

Mom and Dad looked at each other, and Dad shrugged. Were they actually giving in? "Well, I suppose if it's all right with them, then it's all right with us," Mom said, reaching for the salad dressing.

"Oh, I'm sure it'll be okay!" Elizabeth grinned at our parents, then at me. "I'll call Anna and ask her right after dinner."

I snorted in disgust. My parents looked at me in surprise. I covered up by pretending to choke on a bite of lasagna.

"Are you all right, Jess?" Elizabeth asked, looking at me with concern.

I gulped some water and then smiled weakly. "Sure, no problem," I replied. "Just went down the wrong pipe, that's all."

Once I was sure no one was looking, I scowled at my fork. Elizabeth could at least try to hold back her enthusiasm just a little. I mean, spending a week with Anna Wang wasn't like landing on the moon or something. So why was Elizabeth so excited about it when she could be spending the week goofing around in the den with me? Suddenly I felt like I didn't even know my own twin.

Sure, Elizabeth and I had *both* made new friends and developed all these new interests since starting at Sweet Valley Junior High. But now that I thought about it, she'd been hanging out with her friends *all* the time recently. She and Anna were together constantly, and they spent most of their time with Salvador del Valle, also known as El Salvador. He thinks he's some hilarious comedian (he does have his moments)—but he's mostly just severely annoying. On top of that, Elizabeth had also started spending time with this guy Blue Spiccoli and his friends. Blue is this kind of save-the-planet, hug-some-trees nature nut. They met when Elizabeth decided to play intramural volleyball. Volleyball! My twin! Go figure. I never thought she'd be interested in something like that. Reading a book about it, yes. Maybe writing an article about it for *Zone,* the online 'zine she started with her friends. But playing it?

It's like she has so much new stuff in her life, she doesn't even have time for some of the things she used to think were important, I thought, shooting her a sidelong glance. She had this really happy look on her face, like she couldn't wait to ditch me and move in with Anna for a week. Maybe I was one of the things she *used* to think was important.

"Why does it take a whole week to paint our

rooms anyway?" I blurted out, interrupting something my older brother, Steven, was saying about his history class. "I mean, how long can it take to slap a few gallons of paint on the walls?"

"Well, they'll put on a few coats of paint, and each coat has to dry in between. Then the room has to air out for a couple of days." Dad reached over and made this exaggerated show of patting me on the shoulder. "Don't worry, Jessica. The couch in the den isn't *that* lumpy. And you'll have it all to yourself."

I slumped down in my chair, my appetite gone. Sleeping in the den with Elizabeth had seemed like fun. Sleeping there by myself just seemed lame.

Maybe I should stay over with a friend for the week too, I thought, poking at my food with my fork. Then I frowned. Who would I stay with? In the old days the natural choice would have been Lila Fowler, my best friend from Sweet Valley Middle School. But I haven't seen much of Lila this year—we sort of drifted apart when I changed schools. It would be too weird to call her up now, out of the blue, and just invite myself over.

Of course, I did have friends at SVJH. I'd gotten to be pretty tight with Bethel McCoy, one of my track teammates. And then there was Kristin

Seltzer, one of the sweetest, most popular girls in school—I was starting to see her as a real friend these days too. But somehow I couldn't imagine myself spending a whole, entire week with either of them. I couldn't even imagine bringing it up. We weren't the sleep-over kind of friends, at least not yet.

I felt my shoulders slump, realizing the sad, pathetic truth. Paint or no paint, I was stuck by myself at home. I had nowhere else to go.

Elizabeth

"Anna? It's me," I said when Anna answered the phone. "Are you sitting down? Because I have great news."

"What is it?" Anna asked. "Did Salvador finally wash his gym socks?"

I laughed, twirling a strand of blond hair around my finger. "Not quite that good," I admitted. "But still pretty great." I quickly outlined the whole situation, including my idea to stay at her house for the week. "That's if it's okay with you and your folks," I finished at last. "What do you think?"

"That would be great!" Anna said excitedly. "We'll have so much fun! And we can brainstorm tons of ideas for *Zone*. . . ."

"That's what I thought," I agreed. "And maybe we can rent some movies. I've been dying to see *Pool Party II,* and it just came out on video."

"And you could show me how to make those oatmeal-crunch cookies you brought for lunch last week," Anna said.

9

Elizabeth

I was glad that Anna seemed as psyched about a week together as I was. We'd been friends practically from the first day we met. But this would be the perfect chance to do some serious bonding. "Oatmeal-crunch cookies. Definitely," I promised.

Jessica was sitting beside me on the couch, watching TV, and I noticed her shooting me a dirty look. Oops. I *was* being a little loud.

I gave Jessica an apologetic smile and tried to keep my voice down. "Anyway," I said to Anna, "do you think your mom will be okay with it? A week's kind of a long time."

"A week is nothing," Anna declared. "I'm sure she'll say yes. I'll ask her as soon as we get off the phone. Oh! But first, did Salvador tell you about the new song he wrote for his band?"

I switched the phone to my other ear and settled back against the lumpy sofa cushions. "No, tell me." Salvador recently formed a band with a few other friends—Brian Rainey, who works on *Zone* with us; Blue Spiccoli, my friend from volleyball; and Damon Ross, Jessica's boyfriend. They call themselves Big Noise, and the name really fits.

Anna giggled into the phone. "Well, he's very proud of it. It's called 'I Wanna Be Your Twin.' He said you and Jessica were the inspiration for it."

10

"Really?" I wasn't sure whether to be flattered or worried. Some of Salvador's lyrics are really good, but some are kind of goofy. "How does it go?"

"I don't know—he didn't tell me," Anna said. "He was too busy telling me about this other song he wrote called 'I Wanna Be a Teacher.' It's got a verse about each of his teachers, and they're pretty funny. Like for Miss Scarlett, it's about her war against germs. At the end of the verse this giant germ comes marching toward her with a whole germ army behind it, and she faints."

I laughed. Our gym teacher has this major phobia about germs and bacteria. I could only imagine what Salvador could come up with on that topic.

"Which other teachers does he mention?" I asked.

"Well, let's see," she said. "There's Ms. Upton. . . ." Anna went on to tell me as many of the other verses as she could remember. It sounded like Salvador had come up with some pretty funny stuff. That was no huge surprise—he's got a great sense of humor. Of course, some of his teachers don't really see it that way sometimes. And they'd probably be even less impressed if they heard his newest musical masterpiece.

When Anna got to the part about Mrs.

11

Serson, I started laughing so hard, I practically kicked Jessica off the couch. "Oops," I said, pulling my feet up. I'd almost forgotten she was still sitting there. "Sorry about that," I told her, scooting back over to my side.

"Sorry about what?" Anna asked, sounding confused.

"Oh, never mind," I said into the phone. "It was nothing."

Just then Jessica got up and tossed the remote on the coffee table. Without even looking at me, she stomped out of the room—which made me feel a little guilty. I hadn't realized how loud I was getting again. Jessica was probably heading upstairs to watch her show on the set in Mom and Dad's room. *Oh, well,* I thought. *She'll have the TV all to herself for the week while I'm at Anna's. That should make her happy.*

I Wanna Be Your Twin
by Salvador del Valle

I wanna be your twin
So I can borrow your new blue jeans
I'm not too tall or too thin
We're the same—that's what twin means

I wanna be your twin
I wanna be your twin
'Cause we can share everythin'

I wanna be your twin
'Cause then you'd have to hang with me
A best friend all built in
And double the CDs—for free

I wanna be your twin
I wanna be your twin
'Cause we'll have to share everythin'

I wanna be your twin
So we can switch places with each other
When the switching begins
No one will know if it's me or my brother!

I wanna be your twin
I wanna be your twin
Please, won't you be my twin?

Instant Message between Kristin Seltzer and Jessica Wakefield

KGrl99:   Hey, Jessica, whatz up? :-)

WakefieldSV: Hi. Nothing.

KGrl99:   We were just at the mall, and I saw a pair of shorts that screamed your name.

WakefieldSV: Who's "we"?

KGrl99:   I was with Lacey. She was shopping 4 some new shoes.

WakefieldSV: Oh. Right.

KGrl99:   R u sure you're okay?

WakefieldSV: No biggie. Bad mood.

KGrl99:   Uh-oh. :–o Reason?

WakefieldSV: Nothing much. Just my sister being a jerk, that's all.

KGrl99:   Yikes! Want to talk about it?

WakefieldSV: Nah. I gotta go. Sorry. C-ya at school.

Jessica

When I walked into the bathroom to brush my teeth before bed, Elizabeth was already in there, doing the same thing. There are times when it really stinks to share a bathroom with your twin sister. Like when you're trying to ignore her, for instance. That tends to be a lot harder when you're trapped in the same tiny space.

"Oh, I didn't realize you were in here," I said as coldly as I could.

Elizabeth blinked at me over her toothbrush. "*Mwuh?*" she mumbled. Then, holding up one finger, she bent over the sink and spit. "What?"

I shrugged and examined my fingernails. There really wasn't much I felt like saying to her at that moment. And I wanted her to know it.

Elizabeth narrowed her eyes suspiciously. "What's with you? Are you still mad at me for being loud? Please." She shrugged. "Anyway, you wouldn't blame me if you heard . . ."

Before I could stop her, she was off and running

about some totally lame song Salvador wrote about a few of our teachers. I swear, Elizabeth can be totally clueless sometimes. Couldn't she even tell I was *really* mad at her? Didn't she care?

". . . anyway, Anna says she dared him to play it at the next Parents' Night. He said he'd consider it, but only if she dyes her hair green this time." Her eyes sparkled with amusement. Anna had dyed her hair bright red a while ago, and even though it had already washed out, Elizabeth still talked about it like it was the wildest thing anyone had ever done.

I rolled my eyes. "Yeah, right," I said. "Then she should get her eyebrow pierced. Anna is just *so* hip."

Elizabeth frowned, looking confused. "What?"

"Yep," I continued. "And next she'll get a few tattoos and blow off school to go hang out at these crazy underground raves. Really, the excitement never stops when Anna Wang is around. You're so lucky to have such a *cool* friend."

Elizabeth really looked annoyed now. "You don't have to get sarcastic about it," she said stiffly. "It was just a joke. It's not like Anna's going to do it."

"Of course not." I leaned over to check my

reflection in the mirror. The more I thought about it, the more it irked me that my twin would actually choose Annoying Anna over me. What was she thinking? "Dying her hair red was pretty much the limit for her. If she did anything more radical than that, she'd explode."

Elizabeth was still frowning. "What do you have against Anna all of a sudden?"

"Don't get mad at me. I'm just telling it like it is, Liz," I said calmly. "It's not my fault if your friends are kinda, well, boring."

"They're not boring!" Elizabeth crossed her arms over her chest and glared at me. "What are you talking about? You don't even really *know* Anna."

"I don't want to know Anna any more than I already do," I replied. "I have better things to do with my time. Like flossing. Or color coding my socks."

Elizabeth rolled her eyes. "That's so typical," she retorted. "Just because Anna's more interested in writing poetry than shopping, you automatically label her as boring. Well, those are the things I like too. Anna and I have things in common. So maybe we're *both* boring."

"Maybe you are," I shot back.

"You know, you really should get a clue about people, Jess," Elizabeth growled. "Maybe then

17

you'd see that Anna is really smart and fun and nice. She's interesting to talk to and a blast to be around."

I frowned. *I* should get a clue? Well, I was starting to get one. Hearing Elizabeth list Anna's oh-so-wonderful personality points was giving me a strong clue about what my sister looked for in a friend. Obviously Anna had all the right stuff. She was practically perfect. And from the way Elizabeth was scowling at me, she obviously thought I was the total opposite of Anna in every way.

"Whatever," I said, suddenly sick of the whole conversation. "Maybe you should just move in with Anna permanently if you like her so much."

Elizabeth tossed her head. "Maybe I should."

"Fine," I snapped.

"Fine," Elizabeth replied just as coldly.

There was nothing more to say. The bathroom was starting to feel awfully crowded, so I whirled and stomped out, slamming the door behind me. As I did, I heard the door on Elizabeth's side slam too.

18

Jessica Wakefield's Diary

Five Reasons Why I'm Glad Liz Is Gone for the Week

1. I don't have to share the shower with her.

2. She's so uptight.

3. I don't have to pretend to be interested in her boring stories about <u>zone</u> and volleyball and school.

4. I don't have to hang out with her lame friends.

5. I don't have to listen to her criticize me for being shallow.

Elizabeth Wakefield's Diary

Five Reasons I'm Glad to Get Away from Jessica for a Week

1. I don't have to sit around waiting while she hogs the shower.

2. She's so snobby sometimes.

3. I can actually have intelligent conversations, about stuff that actually matters, with Anna.

4. I don't have to listen to Jessica criticize my friends.

5. I don't have to listen to Jessica criticize me for being a boring loser.

Elizabeth

"Hey! Elizabeth!"

I blinked and glanced over my shoulder, wincing at the harsh tone of my twin's voice behind me. "Jess?" Thursday's first lunch period had just ended, and second lunch was about to begin. That always meant a major traffic jam in the halls, especially in the area where we were, right outside the main cafeteria doors. I grudgingly stopped to let Jessica catch up. Maybe she finally wanted to apologize for last night, despite the fact that she'd been ignoring me all morning. I was seriously annoyed about the whole thing, but I guessed I could forgive her if she asked nicely. "What's wrong?"

Salvador and Anna stopped too. "Hey, Jessicat," Salvador said teasingly, rolling his eyes.

Jessica ignored him. That wasn't all that unusual. But her dark, angry expression was. She glared at me. "You're wearing my shirt, that's what's wrong."

I glanced down at the shirt I was wearing. It

was a lavender button-down with embroidered trim. "This?" I said. "But you gave me this shirt. You said it was, and I quote, 'so three months ago.' And anyway, you saw me wearing it this morning. Remember?"

Jessica scowled. "I want it back," she said with a stubborn glint in her blue-green eyes.

I was getting a bad feeling about this. *Is she still mad about that stupid argument last night?* I wondered. *She was obviously the one in the wrong.*

In any case, I wasn't about to get in another fight with her over a shirt—even though she *had* said I could have it. Jessica isn't the most reasonable person in the world when she's angry, and sometimes it's easier just to give her what she wants and wait for it to pass. Besides, I was mad too, and I didn't really feel like making an effort to smooth things over. "Whatever," I said with a shrug. "If you want the shirt back, you can have it back. I'll put it in your room this afternoon."

"I want it back *now*," Jessica snapped. "Before you lose it or ruin it or something while you're hanging out with *Anna*."

"Are you kidding?" I stared at her, feeling a twinge of annoyance. Angry or not, she was acting like a total freak. "It's the middle of the day! And besides, when was the last time I lost or ruined something of yours? It's usually the other way around."

Jessica just glared. "I said I want my shirt back. Now."

What's her problem? I wondered. *It's like she's going out of her way to pick fights with me.*

Our fight last night was pretty bad, but Jessica and I have had a million fights, and most of them are forgotten by the next day. I mean, Jessica isn't exactly the queen of long attention spans. And after I wrote in my diary last night, I felt a lot better. I'd figured I'd probably forgive her sometime today. But now I wasn't so sure I wanted to let it drop. Her attitude was getting severely annoying. It was so unfair for her to rag all over *my* friends just because she was feeling superior. "Why do you want it back?" I demanded. "So you can lose it or ruin it yourself?"

Jessica didn't answer. She just tapped her foot impatiently and stared pointedly at the shirt.

"Hey," Salvador put in, tugging on the hem of his striped rugby shirt. "You can have my shirt if that will help."

Anna swallowed a laugh, but Jessica didn't even seem to hear the joke. She put her hands on her hips. "Fine," she told me sharply. "Keep it if it's so important to you. But that's the last time I ever lend anything to *you*. No matter how much you beg."

That really ticked me off. "You're the one who

walked into my room last week and flung the shirt at me, like I was from some kind of used-clothes garbage dump," I said hotly. "You were the one who said I had to take it because it was poisoning the other clothes in your closet with its uncoolness."

"Whatever." Jessica spun on her heel and stomped off into the cafeteria.

"What's wrong with *her?*" Anna said, staring after my sister in astonishment.

"Yeah," Salvador commented. "It's like she had a personality transplant or something." He shrugged. "Not that she was perfect before. It's like Mr. Hyde and Mr. Hydier."

I glared after her, still steaming over her idiotic tantrum. "I have no idea what's going on with her," I told my friends. "But she'd better get over it soon."

Jessica

"Wakefield! Look alive! We don't have all day."

I blinked, realizing I had totally spaced out and had no idea what Mrs. Krebs, the track coach, had just said. "Uh, sorry," I blurted out, feeling my face getting red. Glancing around, I saw that several of my teammates were lining up on the practice track while the rest were backing off onto the grass nearby. And almost all of them were staring straight at me as if I'd just sprouted an extra nose.

"Jessica!" my friend Bethel hissed, shoving me forward. "You're in this heat. Get out there!"

I shot her a grateful look, then jogged over to take my place at the starting line. Soon there were four of us lined up, hopping up and down to shake off last-minute stiffness. Mrs. Krebs gave a short blast on her whistle, and I crouched in my place, staring straight ahead down the track. I was ready.

The coach counted us off, and I sprang

forward with the others. For the first few yards we were all running in a pack. Then I found my stride and surged forward. *Ha!* I thought in triumph, getting that fantastic feeling of power and freedom that I always got when I was running well. *At least there's one good thing in my life that Elizabeth can't—*

I never finished the thought. At that moment my foot landed wrong somehow, and I stumbled, feeling my ankle wobble and give way to one side, like a loose spring.

"Argh!" I grunted, lurching forward and managing to regain my balance just before I fell. Getting my feet back under me, I gritted my teeth and pounded down the track after the others. This time it didn't feel like I was flying. My breath was ragged, and each footfall made my twisted ankle burn.

I managed to make up some ground, but at the finish line I was still a good five yards behind the next-to-last runner in the heat. I slowed to a stop and leaned over, trying to catch my breath. Then I walked around in a circle a few times, testing my weight on both feet. My ankle throbbed a little, but at least it didn't seem to be broken or even sprained.

"What's your problem, Wakefield?" Bethel asked, tossing me a towel as I limped back to the bleachers to rest as the coach called up the next group. "You looked like you suddenly forgot how your legs worked out there. I hope you don't choke like that in our next meet."

"Give me a break, Bethel," I muttered as I mopped my forehead and neck. "I've got more important things on my mind right now than winning some stupid practice race."

Bethel cocked her head at me, her brown eyes curious. "Oh yeah?" she said bluntly. "This wouldn't have anything to do with your twin sister, would it? I heard you two had some kind of blowup in the hall at lunchtime."

"I don't want to talk about it." I frowned and plopped down on the bottom row of the bleachers.

Bethel stayed right in front of me, doing stretches. "Suit yourself," she said with a shrug. "But remember, a real athlete doesn't let outside stuff get to her when she's in the zone. A real athlete gets the job done no matter what, no excuses."

I felt a flash of annoyance. Bethel could be a little hard to take sometimes—like right now, for instance. Couldn't she tell I wasn't in the mood for a lecture on sportsmanship? First Elizabeth gave me her little speech about what a good friend should be like—I was starting to think of it as the Anna Address. You know, as in, *"Fourscore and seven days ago, the whole world discovered that Anna Wang is perfect and smart and wonderful. . . ."* And now this.

"Can it, McCoy," I snapped. "I don't want to hear it right now, okay?"

"Excuse me?" Bethel drew herself up to her full height and glared at me. Too late, I remembered that she had a pretty quick temper. And she never took any lip from anyone—teammates, teachers, whoever. "Would you like to rephrase that?"

"Whatever," I muttered, leaning over to rub my sore ankle. "I'm just saying."

Luckily at that moment the coach called Bethel's name. After giving me one last glare, she stalked away toward the track.

I let my head fall into my hands. "Great," I muttered. "Just great." All I needed was to start alienating my friends. After all, as Elizabeth had pointed out so helpfully the day before, I didn't have that many to spare.

If I don't watch out, I'm not going to have anyone to hang out with at all, I thought grimly. *And if that happens, it'll all be Elizabeth's fault.*

A n n a

I was a little breathless when I raced into the *Zone* meeting that afternoon. "Sorry I'm late," I panted, seeing that Elizabeth, Salvador, and Brian were already gathered in front of the computer. "Drama club ran long again."

When I saw Elizabeth's grim face, I thought for a second that she was mad at me. When I first joined drama club, I got kind of sloppy about showing up for *Zone* meetings. The others were pretty annoyed about it for a while.

Then Elizabeth smiled at me, and I relaxed. "That's okay, Anna," she said. "But I'm glad you're here. Do you think it would be all right if I came over to your house tonight instead of waiting until tomorrow?"

I shrugged. "Sure, I guess. Why? Are the painters coming early?"

"No." Elizabeth scowled. "I just don't really feel like living under the same roof with Jessica any longer than I have to. She is seriously damaging my mental health."

29

Anna

I exchanged a look with Salvador. Jessica *had* acted like a jerk this morning, but I'd figured she and Elizabeth would have patched things up by the end of the day. "Are you sure that's a good idea?" I asked cautiously. "I mean, maybe you should try to make up with her."

Elizabeth glared at me. "Why should *I* try to make up with *her?*" she demanded. "She's the one who started it. For no reason."

Salvador whistled and held out his hands. "To your corners!" he barked out, like a referee at a boxing match. "Take a breather, and wait for the bell. And no hitting below the belt, or you're outta here!"

Elizabeth rolled her eyes. But I shot Salvador a grateful look. The last thing I wanted to do was make Elizabeth's mood even worse. She's so sweet and good-hearted most of the time, it's kind of scary when she's mad.

"Don't worry," I told her quickly. "I'll check with my mom, but I'm sure it's okay if you want to move in tonight."

"Thanks. I'll have to ask my parents too, but I doubt one night will make a difference." Elizabeth rolled her eyes. "I just don't feel like spending another night with Jessica right now. You saw how she was acting this morning. I'm worried sleeping in the same house with her could be hazardous to my health."

I smiled weakly. I was starting to think the best thing for all of us would be to steer clear of Elizabeth for a while if she was going to be this cranky. *Guess there's not much chance of that for me, though,* I thought. *Not while she's living at my house for the next week.*

Brian cleared his throat. "Okay, then," he said. "Now that that's settled, should we get started? I wanted to get your input on the new design I've been working on for the menu. . . ." He started punching buttons on the computer keyboard.

Salvador made a static noise with his hands. "Begin launch. This is mission control."

I groaned. Salvador practically has a phobia about computers. He should have been born in the eighteenth century. Ever since we decided to turn *Zone* into an online 'zine instead of a regular printed one, he's been cracking *Jetsons* jokes and acting like we're boldly going where no 'zine has gone before.

Ignoring Salvador as he started humming the theme from *Star Trek*, I looked over Brian's shoulder at *Zone*'s main Web page. "Hey!" I said as the images started popping up in their boxes. "That looks really cool, Brian." He'd switched the type around and added some other stuff, like photos and flashing icons. It gave the whole page a much more hip, exciting feel. It was definitely

31

cooler than anything we could have done in old-fashioned printed form.

Elizabeth looked pleased too. "I like it," she declared. "I really think it's—"

"And it's unanimous!" Salvador interrupted, switching into his smarmy-British-announcer voice. "The new design wins by a landslide! It's fab, it's now, it's happening, it's—"

"Salvador!" Elizabeth snapped. "Would you lay off? We're trying to get something done here."

Salvador grimaced. "Sorry, teacher," he said sarcastically. "I was just goofing around."

"You're always just goofing around." Elizabeth's voice was sharp. "Doesn't it ever get old for you? Because it does for me."

This time Salvador actually looked sort of hurt. "Whatever." He stepped back and sat down in a chair a few yards away.

I shot him a sympathetic smile. His smarmy-British-announcer voice was one of my favorites. "Um, so should we talk about new content?" I suggested, trying to cover up the awkward moment. "I was thinking we ought to do some more movie reviews. Maybe one of us could go see *The Getaway*—it opens this weekend, and it's supposed to be awesome."

"Sounds good," Brian spoke up.

Several silent seconds ticked by. Salvador pouted in his chair, Elizabeth stared fixedly at the computer screen, and Brian and I gazed helplessly at each other.

Finally Brian cleared his throat. "You know, I just remembered. I'm supposed to be home early today to, uh, walk the dog. Maybe we should finish this meeting another time. Say this weekend? We could meet at my place Sunday night if you want."

"Sure, okay," Elizabeth muttered darkly. Salvador just shrugged.

I nodded. It seemed like a good idea to get out of there before Elizabeth's foul mood turned on all of us. Besides, it was obvious that we weren't going to get much done today. Salvador was sure to spend the next hour sulking, Brian was clearly feeling totally uncomfortable, and I was afraid to open my mouth. Plus Elizabeth was too focused on her fight with Jessica to think about anything else.

Including the fact that Brian doesn't have a dog.

Note Left in Bethel McCoy's Gym Locker after Track Practice, Thursday Afternoon

Hey, Bethel,
  Sorry about what I said earlier. You were totally right—I was way distracted, totally without focus. Anyway, I'm sorry I snapped at you. I'm just in a bad mood because Elizabeth is being such a jerk lately.
  Forgive me?
  Your friend (I hope),
                    Jessica

Message Left on the Wakefields' Answering Machine, Thursday Afternoon

Beep!

"Hi, this is Bethel McCoy, calling for Jessica. I guess you're not home from practice yet. Anyway, I just got your note. And I guess I'll forgive you, even though you were being a pain. Call me back if you want. Otherwise I'll see you at school tomorrow. Bye!

Beep!

Salvador

I watched a fly buzzing helplessly around the windowsill by my seat on the bus. It kept trying to fly through to the outside, not seeming to realize the glass was in the way. It just kept bumping its little bulgy-eyed head against the hard surface over and over again.

"I know how you feel, buddy," I muttered to the fly.

I noticed an old lady across the aisle giving me a suspicious look. I couldn't really blame her—after all, how many people have conversations with a bug? Still, I couldn't resist making a psycho monster face at her, just to make her think I was even more of a lunatic than she'd imagined.

She frowned, then turned away and sat stiffly facing the window. I grinned, but it didn't make me feel any better. I'd been in a lousy mood since the *Zone* meeting broke up a few minutes earlier.

I was so busy thinking about Elizabeth's

37

mean comments that I almost missed my stop. It wasn't until the bus came to a halt that I glanced out the window and realized we were at the corner near Blue's house.

"Oops," I blurted out, leaping up and almost tripping over the seat in front of me. Instead I ended up just stubbing my toe. "Yeow!" I howled. This time the lady across the aisle wasn't the only one staring. I grinned weakly. "Thank you, thank you," I said loudly. "And now, for my second act, I'm going to make myself disappear." I waved and hurried down the aisle.

Limping slightly, I got off the bus.

When I got to Blue's house, he and Damon were already in the basement, setting up. "Hey, Sal," Blue said when he spotted me coming down the stairs. He ran his hands through his hair and lifted one hand in greeting. "How was your meeting?"

"Does the word *ugh* mean anything to you?" I muttered.

Blue cocked his head, looking concerned. "What happened?"

"It was no big deal," I said, flopping down on a chair. "Elizabeth was just in this totally heinous mood because she got into a fight with Jessica, and she took it out on everyone else. Especially me."

Damon nodded sympathetically. "I hear you," he said. "Jessica's having the same problem. I asked how her day was, and she practically bit my head off. Then she started going off about Elizabeth and didn't stop for at least twenty minutes."

"They're out of control, man." I shook my head in amazement. "The Wakefield twins are at war, but it's the rest of us who are paying the price."

"Tell me about it," Damon said with feeling.

I sighed. "They're acting like total brats to each other. And they're being rude to everyone else all at the same time. It's not fair."

Blue shrugged. "Yeah," he agreed. "But what can you do?"

I don't think he meant it as a question—more like just a comment. But it started me thinking. "What *can* we do?" I mused. "I don't know. But we need to do something."

Damon looked skeptical. "I'm sure they'll make up. They always do," he said. "For one thing, it's only been a day. And anyway, this fight is between Jessica and Elizabeth. It's none of our business."

I scowled. "It *is* our business," I retorted. "Poor Anna has to live with Elizabeth for the next week. And the way the twins were going at it today, there's no way they're going to patch things up for at least that long—especially if they're not living together. I'm sorry, but I can't take another day of Elizabeth like this, much less a week or more." I sat up straight, realizing what a scary thought that was. "I say we put our foot—er, feet—down and stop this before it goes any further."

"What do you have in mind?" Blue asked.

I didn't really have anything in particular in mind. But that had never stopped me before. And I wasn't going to let it stop me now. "I'm going to face this like a man," I declared. "I'm going to head over to the Wakefields' house after practice and make them patch things up. The sooner they stop fighting, the better for all of us."

Jessica

I was home on Thursday night, watching some completely lame show and rubbing my sore ankle, when the doorbell rang. Dragging myself off the couch, I went to answer it.

Salvador was standing on the front step, a goofy smile on his face as usual. "Hey!" he said brightly. "How's it going, Jessicat—er, I mean, Jessica?"

"Oh. It's you. Elizabeth's not here," I said sourly, less than thrilled to see him. At the moment I didn't want to see anyone. "She's staying with Anna, remember?"

"You mean she left already?" he asked, looking worried.

"Do I stutter?" I snapped. I wasn't in the mood for his goofy personality just then. "I just said she wasn't here. Where do you think she went, the planet Neptune?"

"I hear it's lovely this time of year." Salvador grinned.

"Whatever," I muttered, wishing he would get

lost already so I could be alone. That was all I wanted—to be alone with my own miserable self. I hadn't even called Bethel back, though I was majorly relieved that she wasn't still mad at me. In my present mood I was afraid that I'd just wind up ticking her off again if I called. "Now, if you'll excuse me," I told Salvador impatiently, "I have some important TV to watch."

I started to close the door, but he stopped it with his hand. "Wait!" he said, sounding a little desperate. "Um, I mean, can I come in for a second?"

"Why?" I glared at him suspiciously. Salvador and I spent some time together recently trying to help Elizabeth out of a jam. And I'd actually learned he wasn't such a bad guy. But that didn't mean we were best friends now or anything.

He shrugged. "Never mind. We can talk here if you want." He wet his lips, suddenly looking kind of nervous. "I was just wondering. Uh, what's going on? I mean, between you and Elizabeth."

"What are you talking about?" I asked cautiously. I knew Salvador had seen Elizabeth and me fighting this morning, but what made him think I'd want to talk about it with him? And besides, he couldn't know the *real* reason we were fighting. Unless Elizabeth had told him. Which would be just like her.

Salvador put his hands on his hips. "Come on," he said. "I know you two are really mad at each other. What I'm wondering is why?"

"What do you care?" I was really getting annoyed with his nosiness. "What makes you think it's any of your business?"

"Because Elizabeth is my friend." Salvador was starting to look less nervous and more stubborn. "Besides, I don't think she really knows why you're fighting either. At least she hasn't said anything."

I frowned. "It figures," I muttered. I wasn't sure which would be worse—if Elizabeth was just acting like she didn't know why I was mad at her or if she really didn't know. The second possibility would totally prove my point—that she was way too wrapped up with her lame new friends to pay attention to the important things in life. Like her own family, for instance.

"Well?" Salvador said. "Are you going to clue me in or not? Or don't *you* know why you're fighting either?"

With a loud sigh, I gave in. What was the point in hiding it? Besides, Salvador ought to know what kind of fickle, two-faced person he was hanging out with. "If you must know," I told him, "I'm mad because Elizabeth is totally blowing me off for Anna."

43

Salvador wrinkled his forehead, looking confused. "Huh?"

"She didn't even think about staying home and hanging out with me instead of spending the week at Anna's. She practically jumped at the chance to ditch me," I pointed out, frowning as I remembered how quickly she'd come up with the idea of moving in with Anna.

"Oh." Salvador shrugged. "Well, why don't you say something to her? I'm sure she'd be glad to stay home with you if—"

"That's not the point. I shouldn't *have* to say anything. And you'd better not say anything either."

"Okay, fine. But is it so terrible that Elizabeth wants to take a break? I mean, maybe she just wanted a change of scenery."

I rolled my eyes. "El Salvador, you always know just exactly the *wrong* thing to say," I snapped. "It's a rare talent you have."

"No, I mean it," he protested quickly. "It's nothing against you. It's just that she might want to try something new and different. It's like, um, Anna dyeing her hair. It's not that she hated having black hair. She just thought having red hair for a while would be cool."

"Uh-huh." I folded my arms across my chest and glared at him. "Cool. As opposed to uncool. So are you saying I'm uncool?"

He blinked, looking startled. "Uh, no. I mean, um, that's not what I—"

"Fine. I think it's time for you to go home now. Bye."

This time I slammed the door in his face before he could stop me. Then I went back to the den and flopped down in front of the TV again. The soap opera had ended, and an infomercial had started. It was about some thrilling new breakthrough in denture cream.

I sighed. Could my life get any better?

A n n a

"... and then when I got home, there was this message from Jessica written in bright red pen," Elizabeth said with a scowl. "It said, 'I'm still waiting for my shirt. And it better be clean when I get it back.' Can you believe her? She got ink on my pillowcase too. She'll probably say it was an accident, but you know it totally wasn't."

I shrugged weakly, figuring it was finally my turn to speak. "Uh, maybe she—"

"Oh! And then I went to fix myself a snack," Elizabeth interrupted. Her cheeks had two bright red spots on them, like little stoplights glowing on her face. "And we were all out of those chocolate-chip cookies I like. You know, the ones with walnuts? I thought Steven ate them all, like usual, but he told me it was Jessica, and she doesn't even like walnuts. I'm sure she just ate them so I couldn't have them. And then I . . ."

I played with the hem of my pillowcase and

waited for her to wind down. Somehow this wasn't what I'd had in mind when I imagined how this week would be.

Elizabeth was my first real girlfriend. Until she came to Sweet Valley Junior High at the beginning of the year, I'd mostly only hung out with Salvador. He's great, and I couldn't ask for a better best friend in most ways. But I'd sometimes wondered if I was missing out on some, like, *girlie* stuff.

That was one reason I was so excited when Elizabeth called to ask if she could stay with me. This week with her seemed like the perfect chance to make up for lost time. I'd pictured Elizabeth and me hanging out in my room, laughing over silly stuff and talking about new ideas for *Zone*. I'd thought we would also talk about our lives and our friends and stuff and share secrets we'd never told anybody else. It would be sort of like having a temporary sister, one I could really talk to about my dreams and fears and problems—including one particular problem I was having lately. I'd been thinking it would be the perfect time to ask for Elizabeth's advice about Toby.

Toby. I sighed as I thought about him, tuning out Elizabeth's ranting about her twin. Toby and I met in drama club. At my very first meeting he was one of the first people to talk to me and make me feel welcome. Then I got to know him better when he and I were helping a friend from drama club, Larissa, through a tough time. And now we were all going to be in a play together— *West Side Story.* The more I hung out with Toby, the more I liked him. He was funny and warm and friendly, and a really talented actor. Not to mention being incredibly cute, with this sort of springy, curly hair that sometimes seems to have a life of its own. Then there were his eyes . . . and his great smile. . . . Basically I was starting to face the truth—I was developing a major crush on him.

There was just one problem. Larissa.

Tugging on my bangs, I glanced at Elizabeth. She was still talking. Something about the way Jessica chewed her cereal in the morning.

Larissa and Toby and I had been friends for a while. But I knew that Larissa had a severe crush on him. I grimaced as I remembered the glow in Larissa's eyes when she'd confided that to me. At the time I'd thought it was cute. I barely knew either one of them then—all I knew was that they both seemed really nice. I'd thought they'd make a great couple. Now I still thought they were both really nice. Only now the only one I wanted to see paired off with Toby was me.

I remember how terrible it was when I realized that Elizabeth and Salvador liked each other as more than friends and that they'd both been hiding it from me, I reminded myself, thinking back to the early days of our three-way friendship. *I felt so left out, totally betrayed.* Still, my stomach got all twisty and anxious when I thought about Toby and Larissa together. I didn't want to feel that way, but I couldn't seem to help it. And it was getting harder all the time to pretend I just thought of him as a friend.

I don't know what to do to stop feeling this way, I thought helplessly, grabbing my pillow and clutching it to me. *But I do know one thing—I definitely don't want to do anything to hurt Larissa. Especially not when I know how it feels to be in her place.*

Elizabeth paused for breath, and I decided it was time to jump in. "Hey," I said quickly. "I wanted to talk to you about something."

"Huh?" Elizabeth blinked. "Sure. What's up, Anna?"

I smiled with relief. Maybe now we could get off the Jessica-is-a-jerk train and back on the girlie-secrets track. "It's, um, about Toby. You know, the guy from drama?"

"Sure, I know him. Cute guy, curly brown hair, right?" Elizabeth frowned. "Oh, by the way, speaking of hair—did I mention what Jessica told Steven?"

I sighed. Trying to talk to Elizabeth was starting to feel like talking to a brick wall. Actually, the wall would probably be better. At least it wouldn't keep interrupting. "You mean about your headband?" I asked as patiently as I could.

"Uh-huh. Can you believe she accused me of stealing it? I bought that headband with my own money. And just because she pointed it out at the store, she acts like it's half hers. Can you believe that?"

"No," I said. I was becoming more and more convinced that it had been a huge mistake to let Elizabeth stay with me for a whole week. If the next seven nights were going to be this much fun, I might just have to ask her to go home. "I can't believe it at all."

Entry in Anna's Journal, Written in the Bathroom
Late Thursday Night after Elizabeth Falls Asleep

<u>Toby</u>

She sees you
And so do I
Your mouth turned into a smile
We listen to your jokes
She leans on your arm
You smile at each other
You seem to be two
And I am only one

Elizabeth

"Salvador! Over here!" I yelled, waving my hand over the Friday-morning crowds in the hallway.

Salvador waved back, then made his way toward my locker. When he reached me, he smiled sort of strangely. "Hi," he said. "How are you?"

I didn't bother to answer. Instead I reached into my locker and grabbed the shirt I'd worn the day before. It was clean and folded—I'd washed it at Anna's house the night before. "Here," I said, shoving it into Salvador's hands. "Take this."

He blinked down at the shirt in surprise. "For *moi*?" he said. "Thanks, but I don't think it's my size."

"Very funny." I was not in the mood for his jokes right then. "It's Jessica's, remember?" I grimaced. "Actually, technically it's mine—she gave it to me. But since she so rudely demanded it back yesterday, I decided she can have it. I never liked it much anyway."

Elizabeth

"So why are you giving it to me?" Salvador looked confused.

I sighed. He could be really slow sometimes. "You're going to see Damon next period, right? So you can give it to him, and then he can give it to Jessica when he sees her."

Salvador laughed. "This is a joke, right?" he said. "You know where her locker is. Why don't you just give it to her yourself?"

"Because," I said, wishing he could just be serious for once. "I don't want to *see* Jessica, I don't want to *talk to* Jessica, and I definitely don't want to spend any *time* with Jessica until she grows up and gets over herself."

Salvador stopped laughing. "Are you for real?" he said. "Come on, Elizabeth. Don't you think you're taking this ridiculous fight a little far?"

"What?" I scowled at him. Why was he making it sound like this fight was *my* fault? "Jessica's the one who's taking things too far, not me. She's always the one who takes things too far. Besides, she started it."

"Whatever." Salvador ran his hand over his dark hair, looking uncomfortable. "So it's her bad. So what? Is it really worth getting so freaked out about?"

I couldn't believe it. What was so hard to understand here? Jessica had started this fight.

It was up to her to end it. That was the way things worked. If Salvador couldn't see that, I certainly wasn't going to stand around explaining it to him.

"Fine," I snapped, grabbing the shirt back. "If you don't want to help, I'll give it to her myself."

Slamming my locker door shut, I stomped away without waiting for a reply.

Algebra Class, Friday Morning, 10:09 A.M.

Sal,
  Can Elizabeth and I come over to your place and watch videos tonight?
                  Anna

Anna,
  What's the matter, are you afraid to be alone with the evil twin? Ha ha ha!
                  Salvador

Sal,
  Very funny. So can we?
                  Anna

Anna,
  Sure. But you owe me one!
                  Salvador

  P.S. If her head starts spinning all the way around, you're on your own.

Salvador

"What about this?" Damon held up a black denim shirt. "Kind of retro. That could be a cool look for Big Noise."

I glanced at the shirt and shrugged. "It's okay."

I guess Damon noticed that my heart wasn't really in his one-man fashion show because he tossed the shirt back on the shelf and stared at me. "What's with you? It was your idea to come to the mall, and now you're acting like you'd rather be somewhere else."

"It's Elizabeth and Jessica," I grumbled, remembering how Elizabeth had glared at me that morning at her locker. Like it was my fault she couldn't get along with her own twin. "Their stupid fight is really getting old, you know?"

"Tell me about it." Damon sighed and kicked at a loose clothes hanger on the floor nearby. "Jessica is still driving me crazy. All she wants to talk about is Elizabeth. How obnoxious she is, how snotty she is, the works."

I nodded sympathetically. "I feel your pain, dude. Elizabeth has a one-track mind right now too. I think Anna's afraid to be alone with her— she asked if the two of them could come to my place later to hang out."

"You're a brave man." Damon patted me on the shoulder. "I told Jessica I had to baby-sit my little sisters all afternoon just to avoid her."

I shook my head sadly. For some unknown reason, Damon really likes Jessica. If he was making up excuses to stay away from her, she had to be acting just as revolting as Elizabeth was.

"We've got to do something," I said with feeling, thinking back to my pointless talk with Jessica the day before. Now I knew why *she* thought they were fighting, at least sort of. But what good did that do me? She'd asked me not to tell, and it wasn't like Elizabeth seemed too open to working out their problems anyway. I mean, she'd practically freaked on me over that stupid shirt. "Things can't go on like this," I said, shoving my hands into my pockets.

Damon shrugged and leaned against a rack of khaki pants. "What can we do?" he asked, spreading his hands helplessly. "If they want to stay mad at each other, they'll stay mad."

"There must be something we can do," I insisted. "We've just got to use our heads."

I tapped my fingers on the store shelf, thinking hard. Maybe I was going about this all wrong. Talking to the twins separately wouldn't solve anything. The only way to fix things was to get them talking to *each other*. But how could we do that when they weren't even living in the same house?

"We need a decent plan, that's all," I told Damon. "Maybe we could all hang out together and do something both the twins like. That way they'd be forced to be in the same room with each other. They might start talking and make up all on their own if we just give them the chance."

Damon looked interested. "That could work—maybe," he said. "So what could we do?"

"We could go to the bookstore right here at the mall," I suggested. "They're having this author signing tomorrow night—Elizabeth wrote up a notice about it for *Zone*."

"An author signing?" Damon made a face. "That doesn't sound like Jessica's kind of thing. Or mine."

"Ditto for me," I admitted. "Okay, scratch that one. What about bowling? That's always a crowd pleaser."

"I don't know." Damon looked dubious. "I think Jessica's kind of down on bowling these days. She told me the last time she went, she only knocked down, like, three pins and everyone laughed at her."

I grimaced. "Okay, then, what does Miss High Maintenance like to do?"

"She likes to shop," Damon said uncertainly, glancing toward the store entrance. "They're having a big sale at Glamorama this weekend."

"Glamorama?" I snorted. "Yeah, right— Elizabeth hates that place. Anyway, shopping for girls' clothes isn't exactly my idea of a fun-filled Saturday night."

"Well, how about going over to Sweet Valley High tomorrow afternoon to watch their track meet?" Damon suggested. "It's some kind of regional thing. Jessica was talking about it yesterday. Do you think Elizabeth would want to go to that?"

"I don't think so." I stared at Damon as the truth dawned on me. "You know, maybe this is the problem. Jessica and Elizabeth look exactly alike. But aside from that, they have, like, *nothing* in common. They don't like to do the same stuff. They don't like the same music. They're not in any of the same after-school clubs. They don't even have any of the same friends."

Damon scratched his ear. "You're right. It's weird. It's like they're practically opposites in a lot of ways."

"Right. But let's not lose our focus here." I turned and led the way out of the store, deciding a soda and some french fries would help me think. Aiming for the food court, I glanced over at Damon. "The point is, we have to force them to hang out together. Even if it's just at the Cue Café or here at the mall or . . ." My voice trailed off as we turned the corner into the food court. The movie theater was just across the way, and a big sign in front of the entrance caught my eye. It announced that *The Getaway* was opening that very weekend.

"What?" Damon followed my gaze. Then he smiled. "Oh! That's perfect. Jessica told me she's dying to see *The Getaway*."

"Elizabeth just told me the same thing." I pumped my fist a few times, staring at the movie poster. "Yes! We have a plan!"

Jessica

"Stupid thing," I muttered, flinging the remote down on the couch beside me so hard that it bounced up in the air.

"Hey! Watch it!" Steven was sitting at the other end of the couch. "You almost hit me with that."

My dad glanced over the top of his newspaper at me, looking surprised. "What's the matter, sweetie?"

I shrugged. "Batteries are dead," I said. "It figures."

He blinked. "Is something else bothering you, Jessica?" he asked, folding his newspaper. "You don't seem like yourself tonight."

"Never mind," I muttered, wishing I'd just kept quiet. The last thing I wanted to do was explain to my dad that I was bored and lonely and totally miserable and it was all Elizabeth's fault. Not that it wouldn't be nice to have a little sympathy for a change. But if he and Mom heard why I was upset, they'd probably make Elizabeth come home from Anna's house so we could work things out. And that would just make things worse. What would be the point of having them make Elizabeth make up with me? I would just feel even more pathetic.

My dad gazed at me for another second or two, then shrugged and stood up, dropping his paper on his chair. "All right, then," he said. "But I'm here if you need to talk, Jessica. Anyone want popcorn?"

"Sure!" Steven spoke up eagerly. "Extra butter. Oh, and how about a glass of root beer? And maybe some chips and that bag of cookies."

"Why don't you just ask him to drag the whole refrigerator in here?" I started making oinking noises, but somehow it didn't seem as amusing as usual.

Dad shook his head at us, then left for the kitchen. Giving up on the remote, I stood and walked over to the TV, switching the channels until I stumbled across a music video. I glanced over my shoulder, expecting Steven to protest. But he was grinning at me.

"What's your problem?" I demanded.

"So what was it this time?" he asked with a smirk. "I know it's not just the paint fumes getting to you. Did Elizabeth borrow your lip gloss without asking? No, wait—let me rephrase that.

Did *you* borrow *her* lip gloss without asking, accidentally flush it down the toilet or something, and then ask her to use her own money to buy you a new one to replace it?"

I made a face at him. "Very funny."

"Come on, spill," Steven wheedled. "I heard you two arguing in your bathroom the other night. What gives? What'd you do to make her so mad?"

"What makes you think this was *my* fault?" I snapped, irritated. "For your information, Elizabeth started it."

"Oh yeah? What'd she do?"

Before I could answer him, the phone rang. A second later Mom called my name from upstairs. "It's for you!"

I blinked, wondering for a second if it could be Elizabeth. *Maybe she finally realized how she's been acting,* I thought hopefully, grabbing the phone. *Maybe she's calling to tell me how wrong she was and she's coming straight home. . . .*

"Hello?" I said.

"Jessica? Hi, it's Damon."

I slumped, a little disappointed. This was probably the first time since we'd started dating that I wasn't happy to hear Damon's voice on the other end of the phone line. "Hey," I said, trying to sound normal. "What's up?"

"I just found out *The Getaway* opens at Cinema 6 this weekend. Want to go tomorrow night? We could meet there at six-thirty."

That snapped me out of my rotten mood, at least a little. "Sure!" I said eagerly. "You know I'm dying to see that."

"Great! Um, Kaia is running around the house with her shorts on her head and I have to go catch her, so I can't really talk. But I'll see you tomorrow, okay?"

"Okay. Bye, Damon."

I hung up the phone, suddenly feeling a lot better about life in general. Who needed Elizabeth anyway? A cute guy, a great movie—it was the perfect way to take my mind off my troubles.

Now all I had to do was survive the next twenty-four hours.

Elizabeth

"I hope he likes the movies you—uh, I mean, *we*—picked out," Anna said, sounding worried. "Salvador doesn't usually like movies with subtitles that much."

I stepped forward and rang Salvador's doorbell. "Well, he'll just have to deal," I said, clutching a bag of videos. "You can't let people get away with bossing you around all the time and acting like babies when they don't get their way."

Anna bit her lip. For some reason, she looked sort of worried. But I shrugged it off. So what if foreign films weren't Salvador's favorite? Sometimes people had to accept things that they didn't like. That was life. Anyway, I was in the mood for some culture. I could never have watched a foreign film at home. One time I rented this movie *Babette,* and Jessica spent the first twenty-five minutes pretending to barf over the side of the couch. Then she'd pressed the stop button and

Elizabeth

started dancing around in front of the TV until I agreed to watch something else instead. Typical.

The front door opened, interrupting my train of thought. Salvador's grandmother smiled at us. "Hello, girls," she said. "Come on in—Salvador's in the living room."

"Thanks." I walked in, and Anna followed, clutching the boxes from the video store. Salvador lives with his grandmother—he calls her the Doña—because his parents are in the military and they travel constantly. The Doña is really cool even though she's a grandmother. She takes all these classes, like fencing and ballroom dancing and stuff like that.

You know, even as cool as his grandmother is, I always thought it would be really hard to be in Salvador's place, I thought idly as the Doña headed back toward the kitchen. Delicious smells were wafting out of there, and I guessed she was practicing what she'd learned in one of her gourmet-cooking classes. *I mean, having your parents all the way on the opposite side of the world seems so harsh. On the other hand, if it was, say, your twin sister who was living off in Tahiti or somewhere, that would be a totally different story. . . .*

Salvador was watching a cartoon when we

walked in. "Hi," he greeted us, hitting the mute button on the remote. "So what'd you guys get? Was *Pool Party II* in?"

"No, it was already checked out," Anna replied.

"Rats! I knew we should have reserved it." Salvador looked disappointed. Then he shrugged. "Oh, well. So what did you get instead? *Fists of Fire? Danger in Space?*"

Anna glanced over at me. Then she turned back toward Salvador and smiled weakly. "We got these." I tossed the videos onto the couch beside him.

Salvador picked up the boxes and read them. "Huh?" He wrinkled his nose. "I've never even heard of these."

"They're supposed to be excellent," I said, taking one of the boxes back and popping out the cassette. "This one's about the resistance movement during World War II."

Salvador held up his hands. "Wait a minute," he said. "I think there's some confusion here. You got World War II. I wanted *Pool Party II*. You know—fun in the sun, splashing, jokes. Not death and destruction. Well, not unless the death and destruction take place somewhere interesting, like outer space."

"Not everything in the world is fun and

jokes," I reminded him. "You need to realize that, Salvador. Anyway, I want to see this. It won a ton of awards when it came out."

Anna looked nervous. "Um, it's probably good," she said. "I mean, it might be interesting to see a different kind of movie this time."

Salvador was gritting his teeth. I could tell he was less than thrilled about my choice of videos. *So what?* I thought, checking to make sure the tape was rewound. *He always gets to pick what we watch. He doesn't need to get all upset because I decided to pick something I want to see for a change.*

I stuck the tape into the VCR. I was sort of expecting him to argue—maybe insist on going back to the store to exchange the videos or watching cartoons instead. Or at least make jokes about the movie I picked.

But he just cleared his throat and smiled faintly. "Okay," he said. "I guess it'll be interesting. Um, but speaking of movies, I just remembered—*The Getaway* is opening this weekend. How about if we all go tomorrow night?"

"Sure!" Anna said immediately. "That sounds like fun, Sal. Doesn't it, Elizabeth?"

I smiled. "Definitely," I said. "*The Getaway* is supposed to be great. I'll be there."

Elizabeth

"We could meet in front of Cinema 6 at six-thirty," Salvador said.

I nodded and sat down on the couch beside Anna and hit the play button on the remote. "Sounds good," I said, relaxing. "Now, come on, let's start this thing."

Jessica Wakefield's
Friday Night as a Loser

6:45 P.M. Jessica asks for a second helping of squash, just so she has an excuse to stay at the dinner table with her family. Steven nearly chokes on his apple juice in amazement—Jessica hates squash! He suggests that their parents take her temperature in case she's coming down with something.

7:05 P.M. Jessica spends five minutes arguing with Steven over the remote—she wants to watch music videos; he wants to watch the all-sports station. The argument is settled when Mr. Wakefield enters and announces that they're going to watch the stock-market report.

7:24 P.M. Jessica's eyes are glazed over and her mind is numb from watching the stock-market report with her father. The only good part about it is that Steven gave up and left the room. Aha! Now she can watch videos in peace.

7:42 P.M. Steven walks into the den. Jessica prepares to resume their battle over the remote. But it turns out Steven is just there looking for his car keys. He has a date. Knowing that her dorky older brother has a better social life than she does depresses Jessica more than anything she could have imagined.

8:12 P.M.   Jessica is tired of watching TV. She considers calling Kristin or Bethel but decides against it. She doesn't want them to know that she's sitting around home alone on a Friday night. Besides, if she finds out they're both out, she knows she'll really feel like the queen of dorks.

9:28 P.M.   Jessica has already taken a shower, deep conditioned her hair, given herself a facial, and filed her nails. She wonders how early she can go to bed without being considered a total loser.

9:55 P.M.   When she finds herself actually picking up her algebra book and considering whether she should start her weekend homework, Jessica knows she has hit rock bottom. She flings her algebra book into the hallway, and crawls into her temporary bed in the den, relieved that the whole lousy day is just about over.

10:07 P.M. Mrs. Wakefield walks past the den on her way to the kitchen. She stops short in surprise, seeing that Jessica is already in bed. Jessica assures her that she's feeling okay, she doesn't have a fever, and nothing is wrong. Pretending to be exhausted, she yawns loudly and rolls over to face the wall.

11:58 P.M. Jessica wakes up when Steven comes in from his date and trips over her algebra book. She groans and pulls the covers up over her head, wondering why the funniest things happen when she's just not in the mood.

Jessica

I glanced at my watch for about the millionth time in the past ten minutes. "Where is he?" I muttered under my breath.

Turning slowly on my heel, I scanned the crowds milling around in front of the movie theater. A couple of ninth-grade guys were just heading inside, and a pair of kids from the drama club were at the end of the long line at the box office. Other than that, I didn't see anyone I recognized. Specifically, I didn't see Damon.

Sighing loudly, I checked my watch again. Six-forty. I hated standing there alone, looking like I had no friends. It wasn't like Damon to keep me waiting, but with the way things were going lately, I wouldn't be surprised if it turned out he'd asked me to meet him the next night and I'd mixed up the dates.

When I glanced around for him again, my jaw dropped open and my eyebrows shot up. "Elizabeth?" I blurted out, spotting her rounding the corner with Anna. "What are *you* doing here?"

She looked as surprised to see me as I was to see her. And almost as happy about it. In other words, *not*.

"I'm here to meet my *friends,*" she said icily. "Anna and I were just looking for Salvador—he's supposed to be meeting us here, and he's late. What are *you* doing here?"

"I'm meeting Damon," I replied, keeping my voice just as cold. "Not that it's any of your business." I glanced around again, praying for Damon to arrive and rescue me.

He was nowhere in sight, so I looked back at Elizabeth. She was scowling. Beside her, Anna was cringing and glancing around like she wanted to be anywhere else but there. I couldn't blame her. Elizabeth was acting like a total jerk.

"By the way," I said sarcastically, "thanks *so* much for giving my shirt back. I only had to iron it ten times to get all the wrinkles out after you stuffed it in my locker."

"Yeah, right." Elizabeth snorted. "Don't you mean *Mom* had to iron it? I didn't think you even knew we owned an iron. You certainly never use it after you borrow *my* clothes."

I folded my arms across my chest and glared at her. "Your clothes?" I said. "Why would I want to borrow any of your clothes? It's not even close to Halloween."

"Um, excuse me," Anna muttered. "I just noticed that Larissa and Toby are over there in line. I'm going to go say hi." She scurried away without a backward glance.

Elizabeth hardly seemed to notice her friend's quick exit. She was too busy giving me the evil eye. "You know, I'm glad the painters kicked us out of our rooms," she snapped. "It's nice to be spending the week living with someone who's not so rude and obnoxious."

"It takes one to know one." It wasn't exactly a brilliant response, but Elizabeth was making me so mad that I couldn't really think straight. How dare she call me rude and obnoxious? She was the one who had decided to blow me off and act like she couldn't wait to get away from me.

I looked at my watch. It was a quarter to seven. Where was Damon anyway?

Elizabeth noticed what I was doing. "What's wrong?" she asked sarcastically. "Am I boring you?"

"As a matter of fact, yes," I snapped, fed up with her attitude. Why was she getting in my face? I was the one who should be mad, not her. "I'm totally bored with this whole conversation."

"Oh, really? I was just about to say the same

Jessica

thing." Elizabeth checked her own watch. "So don't let me keep you."

She looked so smug, I wanted to strangle her. Instead I clenched my fists at my sides so I wouldn't explode. "Fine," I said through gritted teeth. "I'm out of here. If Damon ever bothers to show up, tell him I went home."

I spun on my heel and marched away as fast as I could because I felt like I might burst into tears at any second. And I *definitely* didn't want to give Elizabeth the satisfaction of seeing me cry.

Salvador

"It's about time!" an angry voice exclaimed as Damon, Blue, and I rounded the corner from the theater parking lot. Blue's brother had dropped us off there on his way to meet some friends. Actually, he'd dropped us off like twenty minutes earlier. But we'd hung out in the parking lot for a while, giving the twins time to find each other and make up. Judging by the fact that Jessica was nowhere in sight and Elizabeth looked like some kind of enraged wild animal, I was guessing things hadn't gone quite the way we'd hoped.

I gulped and glanced at the other guys. "Uh-oh," I muttered under my breath. Then I turned to face Elizabeth, trying to look apologetic. "Hi," I said. "Um, sorry we're late."

Elizabeth's blue-green eyes were practically shooting flames. "Late?" she screeched. "It's almost ten to seven! You were the one who told us to be here at six-thirty, remember? So where were you?"

I exchanged a quick glance with Damon and Blue, wondering what to say. My plan hadn't gone quite this far. I'd figured that by the time we showed up, Elizabeth and Jessica would be best buds again and we wouldn't need an excuse. In fact, I'd sort of imagined them thanking us for our efforts. Fat chance. "Um—Um . . . ," I stammered, not sure how to respond. My first instinct was to scream and head for the hills, but I seriously doubted that would do anyone much good.

"Well?" Elizabeth tapped her foot, looking sort of the way Ms. Upton does when we're late for class. Only scarier. All Ms. Upton does when she's mad is give me detention. Elizabeth looked capable of doing a lot more damage than that.

I wet my lips, which were strangely dry all of a sudden. "Where's Anna?" I asked, stalling for time.

Elizabeth blinked, looking confused for a second. Then she glanced toward the line outside the ticket office. Most of the audience was inside already, waiting for the movie to start. But there were a few people still waiting in line.

"She's over there." Elizabeth waved a hand toward the small group.

I glanced over and spotted Anna talking to

Toby and Larissa. Then I glanced at Damon nervously. So far, it looked like our plan was a total bust. "Uh, where's Jessica?" I blurted out.

"Jessica?" Elizabeth's eyes narrowed suspiciously. "How did you know she would be . . . Oh!" She nodded grimly. "I get it."

"Uh, get what?" I asked as innocently as I could.

She put her hands on her hips and glared from me to Damon and back again. "You two planned this, didn't you?" she demanded. "You were trying to make me and Jessica run into each other."

I grinned weakly. "Well, sort of," I admitted. There didn't seem to be much point in hiding the truth any longer. I should have known she would figure things out soon enough. "But only because we thought you guys would make up if you just had the chance to talk to each other."

"Make up?" Elizabeth repeated. "This isn't about that. This whole thing will be over once Jessica apologizes because it's all her fault."

Damon was shaking his head. "Oh, really?" he spoke up. "Because that's exactly what Jessica is saying about you."

I nodded, remembering what Jessica had said to me the other day. "Right," I said. "So why can't the two of you just admit it's *both* your faults and get on with your lives?"

"Sounds like a plan," Damon said. "I'm going to look for Jessica."

As he loped off, Elizabeth turned to me. "I don't care what Jessica says. I already told you— it's *her* fault, not mine." She had this stubborn look on her face. That expression was getting really familiar, and I was sick of it. To tell the truth, I was getting a little sick of Elizabeth too.

"Whatever," I snapped. "I'm going to catch up with Anna." I felt bad about leaving Blue alone with Elizabeth, but I couldn't take it anymore. I hurried off toward Anna, Toby, and Larissa without a backward glance.

A n n a

"Wow," Salvador said, interrupting a story Larissa was telling about life in London. "This is great. It's so nice to hang out with normal people again!"

"Normal?" Toby made a funny face as he held open the theater door for the rest of us to walk through. "We've never been called that before, have we, Larissa?"

She giggled. "Take it back, you fiend!" she said, giving Salvador a playful shove.

I laughed too. "I think he means he's glad you're not the Wakefield twins," I explained. "The two of them are mad at each other—like, *demented* mad—and being around them is like being in a war zone."

"Right," Salvador broke in. "Only less relaxing."

Poking him on the shoulder, I laughed again. "Anyway, we've been trying to help them through this, but it's like they don't even notice we're around."

Larissa nodded sympathetically. "I hear you,"

she said as she led the way toward an empty row of seats. The theater was pretty crowded already. "It's hard to feel close to a friend when they're totally wrapped up in their own issues."

I gulped and sneaked a peek at Toby. Larissa's words reminded me of my own problems. *Tell me about it,* I thought nervously as I followed Salvador down the row. Toby was right behind me, and I was very aware of how close he was. *Maybe Elizabeth hasn't been the greatest friend in the world lately, but I'm just as bad—if not worse. I've been obsessing over Toby so much that it's making me feel weird to be around Larissa. Like I'm betraying her because I can't help thinking about the guy she likes.*

Glancing over, I noticed that Larissa hadn't followed Toby into our row. She was checking her watch. "I'll be back in a jiff," she said. "I want to head to the loo before the movie starts."

I'd been hanging around Larissa enough to know that *loo* meant bathroom. It was one of the funny British words she always used since she'd spent so much time living in England. She had the greatest accent too, which made words like *loo* sound extra funny. "Okay," I said, trying to sound normal. "We'll save your seat."

"Okay, then," Larissa said, looking back and

forth between Toby and me. With a little wave she headed off toward the lobby.

I winced, thinking how her face glowed. *She really likes Toby a lot,* I thought. *And no wonder. They're both supernice; they have tons in common. . . .*

"Hey, Anna." Toby's voice interrupted my thoughts. "Did you see the set the crew is building for the play?"

I nodded. Earlier that week the stage crew for *West Side Story* had taken over the back of the theater, putting together the huge backdrop that would make up the rear wall of the stage. "The set is going to be . . . interesting," I said, not sure what to say. Personally, I thought the set was really strange looking. But I didn't want to say so in case Toby liked it.

He cocked an eyebrow at me. "Interesting?" he repeated.

Salvador leaned over and grinned at him. "That's not what she called it yesterday," he reported. "She said it looked like a spaceship landing on a plate of muffins."

"Sal!" I elbowed him in the ribs, mortified. For all I knew, the set was some kind of cutting-edge theatrical design. I was still pretty new to this whole drama thing—I didn't want Toby to think I was totally clueless.

But Toby laughed. "A spaceship landing on a plate of muffins!" he hooted. "That's perfect. It's obvious you're a poet, Anna. You really have a way with words."

I blushed and laughed, relieved. "Thanks. It just came to me when I saw it."

"I'm not going to be able to look at it again without cracking up," Toby declared. "Or feeling hungry."

I giggled. "I'd like my stage set with a big glass of OJ, please."

"I'll take coffee with mine," Toby responded. "Black, so I'll be good and alert when the aliens land."

"Hi! What's so funny?"

I glanced over and saw that Larissa had just taken her seat on Toby's other side. I gulped. I hadn't even noticed her return. "Oh, um . . . We were just talking about the new set for the play."

"What about it?" Larissa smiled expectantly.

"We were just saying that it looks, um, kind of strange," I said.

"Anna said it looked like muffins—uh, I mean, a spaceship—uh, never mind. You kind of had to be there, I guess." Toby elbowed me in the side. "And you probably had to be hungry too. Right, Anna?"

"Oh." Larissa didn't say anything else, but I

couldn't help noticing she looked sort of hurt as Toby started laughing again.

I winced, feeling terrible. *Looks like I was right,* I thought, sinking down into my seat and grabbing a handful of Salvador's popcorn. *Elizabeth's definitely not the only slacker of a friend around here these days.*

Jessica

"Stupid phone!" I hollered, giving the pole the pay phone was mounted on a swift kick.

My big toe connected solidly with the wooden pole, and I immediately realized my mistake in kicking at it with sandals on. And with the same foot I had already injured in track practice, no less. Shrieking with pain, I hopped around the movie theater's parking lot in agony. When had my life become so totally pathetic? I wiggled my toes, making sure I could still move them.

"Jessica?" an uncertain voice said.

Gulping, I glanced over and saw Damon walking toward me from the direction of the theater doors. *Yikes,* I thought. *It figures he'd catch me at the very second when I'm hopping around like an idiot. Now he'll probably want to dump me, to make my life totally perfect.*

"Hi," I said, my face flaming.

I dropped my foot and did my best to stand

up straight, though I couldn't help wincing. My toe injury was superpainful, and my ankle was throbbing again. But none of that was as disturbing as the thought of how immature I must have looked to Damon right then.

"Um, I was just trying to call my brother to come pick me up," I explained, desperately trying to maintain whatever dignity I had left. "I just used my last quarter, but there's still no answer, and the phone ate my money."

"Oh." Damon didn't say anything else for a few seconds. Instead he dug into his jeans pocket and fished out several coins. He held out his hand. "Here."

I picked out three quarters and smiled weakly at him. "Thanks."

Then Damon sat down on the curb near the phone and patted the cement beside him. "Want to talk about it?"

"Not really," I muttered. But I perched carefully next to him, smoothing my skirt and wriggling my toe. The feeling was starting to come back. Unfortunately, most of the feeling was icky and painful.

"So?" Damon said after several seconds of silence. "What's this all about, Jess? I mean really."

I looked at him. His gorgeous eyes looked

concerned and confused. "What do you mean?" I asked cautiously.

"I mean you and your sister," he replied. "You guys are really taking it to the mat. At least that's what it looks like from where I'm standing."

"It's no big deal," I said with a shrug. "Elizabeth and I fight all the time."

"But not like this."

I wondered how he knew that. After all, I'd only known him for a few months. Still, that was Damon for you—he always kind of saw right through things and understood stuff I hadn't even told him. That was one of the reasons I liked him. "You're right," I admitted. "We haven't been this mad at each other for a long time. But it's all her fault!"

"What did she do to you anyway?" Damon asked curiously, leaning his elbows on his knees.

"Don't get me started." I sighed, thinking back to Wednesday night at dinner. The excited look on Elizabeth's face when she asked if she could stay with Anna all week. The feeling in the pit of my stomach when I realized my own twin had no interest in bunking with me for a few days. "She dissed me, that's what," I told Damon bitterly. "And the worst part is, she doesn't even seem to realize it."

"You mean this is about Elizabeth deciding to

stay at Anna's?" Damon asked, seeming surprised.

"Of course," I said. Then I bit my lip, realizing for the first time that maybe there was a teensy bit more to it than that. "And I guess it's also about some other stuff," I added reluctantly. "Like the fact that in the old days, I would've been the one blowing her off and not the other way around."

"What do you mean?"

I sighed, wondering how to explain it. "Back at Sweet Valley Middle School—you know, before we got rezoned—I was always the one with tons of friends and lots of stuff to do all the time. If this were happening back then, I probably would've been the one to jump at the chance to stay with my best friend, Lila, or one of our other friends. And Liz would have been the one stuck at home on the lumpy old sofa bed."

"So why don't you just do the same thing now?" Damon asked. "Why don't you ask Kristin or Bethel or someone if you can stay at their house? Then it won't matter what Elizabeth does. You can both be happy."

I picked at a loose thread on my skirt, ashamed to admit the answer. "I—I just don't think I can do that," I said softly. "I'm not sure I'm that close with my friends here. Not yet anyway." I sneaked a peek at his face out of the corner of my eye. Would admitting that make me seem like a loser? Would it make Damon not want to hang out with me anymore? But he just looked thoughtful. "Well, what about your old friends? Lisa, was it? Could you call her? See if she wants to hang out?"

"It's Lila." I shrugged. "And I don't think that would work either. Ever since school started this year, we haven't really kept in touch. She's busy with her life at SVMS, and I'm busy too."

Right. I was busy. Busy trying to fit in with a bunch of people who hardly knew I was alive. Busy figuring out where I fit in. Busy realizing my whole life had changed. I wasn't about to say any of that stuff to Damon, though. I sounded pathetic enough as it was.

Still, it felt kind of good to talk to him. He actually seemed to understand and sympathize with what I was going through. This was the kind of chat I usually only ever had with Elizabeth. When we were speaking to each other, that was.

I frowned, thinking about that. "The worst part is," I blurted out, "Liz used to be the one person I could count on. You know, to be there for me. To always put me first. And now she's so wrapped up with all her new friends . . ." I realized my voice sounded kind of bitter, but I couldn't help it.

"That's a bummer," Damon agreed quietly. "But I'm sure that underneath it all, you're still number one with her. Maybe you're a little jealous that Elizabeth has all these new people in her life. It's kind of like with me and my mom's boyfriend. I really wasn't sure I—"

"What?" I interrupted, hardly hearing whatever he was saying about his mom. "You think I'm jealous of Elizabeth? *Me?*"

So much for Damon understanding what I was going through! He didn't understand a thing. That wasn't what I was saying at all, and besides that, he still seemed to think this was somehow my fault. That it was *my* problem that my own twin barely knew I existed anymore.

I jumped up, suddenly furious. "I can't believe you're taking her side!" I yelled, wincing as I put weight on my injured toe. "I thought you understood. But I guess the joke's on me. *Nobody* understands. Not anymore."

Glancing around, desperate to escape—from Damon and Sweet Valley Junior High and my whole miserable life—I spotted the sign for the rest rooms. I whirled around and raced for the women's room inside, barely hearing Damon calling my name behind me.

Contents of Jessica Wakefield's Purse, Which She Digs Through in the Women's Bathroom at Cinema 6 to Occupy Herself Until She's Sure Damon Is Gone

One packet of cinnamon-flavored gum
Three lip glosses: one Perfect Peach, one Cool Coral Reef, and one Mulberry Delight
SVJH student ID card
One pen cap
Two pens
Fourteen dollars and five cents, plus one Canadian penny
A discount coupon good at Music Mania, expiration date last Thursday
Mrs. Wakefield's business card, slightly crumpled
A broken shoelace from her running shoes
One comb, three ponytail bands, and two barrettes
A photo-booth snapshot of herself and Elizabeth, taken the year before on their birthday. They both look happy.

Blue

"What do you think they put in this popcorn butter anyway?" I held up a kernel and inspected it in the light of the overheads. Then it started to drip buttery goo on my shirt, so I popped it in my mouth.

"Huh?" Elizabeth glanced over at me, looking distracted. "Did you say something?"

I shrugged and smiled at her. She looked pretty cute when she was mad. Her cheeks were flushed pink, and there was a fiery look in her blue-green eyes. "I was just wondering about the butter." I fished another especially buttery piece out of the popcorn bucket on my lap. "See? This color doesn't exist in nature."

Elizabeth blinked at the popcorn blankly. Then her mouth twitched. "Sure, it does," she said. "It's the exact shade of a giraffe. You know, the parts between the spots."

I laughed. "Hey, you know, you're right," I exclaimed, tossing the popcorn in my mouth and crunching. "Maybe this is material for a major exposé in that 'zine of yours."

She giggled. "Maybe."

"Here." I held out the popcorn bucket toward her. "Have some giraffe."

"Thanks." She grabbed a handful and smiled at me.

I grinned back. Now we were getting somewhere. I was still kind of amazed that we were sitting there together. After the smack down with her twin outside, Elizabeth had been ready to blow off the movie and go home. But somehow I'd changed her mind. The theater was almost full when we got inside, but we'd found a couple of seats near the back.

"So," I began cautiously. I felt like I had to bring up the topic of the big twin feud. Salvador and Damon weren't having much luck bringing the two sides together, so I figured it was my turn to give it a shot. "Major scene out there just now. You know, with your sister."

Elizabeth sighed and glanced over at me. "I hate fighting with Jessica," she admitted, reaching for more popcorn. "It's just that she's being so unfair. I can't just let it slide."

"I hear you," I said. "Being related to someone who's also a friend can sometimes be a drag."

I was thinking about my older brother when I said it. Leaf has been my whole family ever since our folks died when I was a kid. He also happens to be one of the coolest people I've ever known. But even so, we don't always get along perfectly.

"Leaf and I have had some knock-down-drag-outs over the years," I told Elizabeth. "But it's usually just because we care about each other so much, you know? Like, you always get ticked off at the ones you love."

Elizabeth nodded uncertainly. "Sure," she said. "Jess and I have been through that kind of stuff too. But this is different."

"Are you sure?" I asked with a shrug. "I mean, maybe this is all a big misunderstanding. Maybe you sort of, you know, unintentionally hurt her feelings or something. That's usually what this stuff is about. And that could explain why she's acting like such a jerk."

I was pretty proud of that conclusion. But Elizabeth didn't seem quite as impressed with my great insight as I was.

"What are you saying?" she snapped, her blue-green eyes clouding over with suspicion. "You're saying this is *my* fault? That I did something to provoke Jessica to walk all over me? I can't believe you're actually *defending* her! I don't need this!"

I opened my mouth to protest. That wasn't what I was saying at all.

But it was too late. She jumped up so fast, she knocked over the popcorn, and took off for the exit.

Jessica

I shoved open the bathroom door so hard that it almost crashed into someone standing near the sinks inside. I'd just gone out to try calling Steven again, but there was no answer. Luckily I'd made it to the phone and back without running into Damon or anyone else I knew, but I wasn't taking any chances. I planned to hide out in the bathroom until I tracked down my stupid brother and got him to come pick me up. "Oops!" I said, peering around the door. "Sorry about that. I—"

My voice cut off as I realized the person I'd almost creamed was Elizabeth. She was checking her hair in the mirror.

"Oh," I said coldly. "It's you. Never mind."

She glared at me. Then she spun on her heel without a word and stalked toward the two rickety stalls set side by side across from the sinks. She disappeared inside the closest one, and I heard the latch snap shut.

Jessica

I rolled my eyes. *Fine,* I thought. *If she's going to be that way, I'll play along.*

I stomped into the second stall. I had to go to the bathroom anyway. And if I took my time about it, I wouldn't have to see her obnoxious face when she came out again.

So far, this was shaping up to be one of the most pathetic nights of my life. Or at least my life since transferring to Sweet Valley Junior High. Why did so many things have to change at once? It didn't seem fair that for the past few months, I had had to adjust to a new school, make new friends, *and* deal with my twin's new superior, social-girl personality all at once.

I was so busy thinking about all the changes in my life that I didn't notice until too late that my stall was all out of toilet paper. *Great,* I thought, rolling my eyes. *That just puts the cherry on top of this whole lousy evening.*

I cleared my throat, knowing what I had to do. I didn't like it, but what choice did I have? "Elizabeth?" I said. "Um . . . Could you pass me some paper? I'm all out over here."

There was no immediate response, and for a second I was afraid she was going to ignore me. Then I heard rustling, and a second later a hand popped under the divider between the stalls, holding a generous helping of tp.

"Thanks," I said, taking it.

A few seconds later I let myself out of the stall. Elizabeth was emerging from hers at the same time.

She gave me a tentative smile. "You're welcome," she said softly as she turned to the sink to wash her hands.

I couldn't help smiling back as I stepped over to the other sink. Did this mean Elizabeth was sorry for treating me so badly? Maybe all she needed was a nudge from me. If she would just apologize, I could forgive her and then we could get back to our normal lives.

"So," I said cautiously, grabbing a paper towel to dry my hands. I glanced at her over my shoulder. "Some night, huh?"

Elizabeth gave a slight laugh. "Yeah," she said. "Our friends set us up, you know, getting both of us to the movies tonight. They were out of line, but I guess they were just trying to be helpful."

So that's why Damon was so late, I realized.

I tossed my paper towel into the overflowing wastebasket. Then I turned toward Elizabeth and smiled encouragingly, waiting for her to go on. I figured this was the point where that apology could just slip out naturally into the conversation.

But Elizabeth didn't say anything else. I cleared my throat. "Okay, then," I said expectantly. "Um . . ."

"Look, Jess." Elizabeth took a step toward me. "I know you hate having to admit you're wrong and saying you're sorry. I just want you to know that it's okay. I forgive you for the way you've been acting."

"*You* forgive *me?*" I exclaimed, wondering if I'd heard her wrong. "Better check that memo again! Because unless I'm sadly mistaken, *you're* the one who ought to be apologizing!"

"Are you clinical?" Elizabeth frowned. "Why should I apologize? You're the one who's been acting like a total jerk!"

My jaw dropped. I couldn't believe her nerve. After all this, was she still so totally clueless?

"*Argh!*" I exclaimed, fed up. Spinning around, I shoved open the bathroom door and stomped out.

So much for that, I thought grimly as I stalked toward the parking lot to try Steven one more time.

Glancing over my shoulder, I was just in time to see Elizabeth slipping back into the theater, where the movie must have already started. She was probably going inside to meet up with her best buddy, Anna.

Jessica

I sighed and fished the last two quarters Damon had given me out of my pocket. The first one went straight through to the coin return with a clunk.

Who needed a twin sister anyway?

Instant Message between Brian and Salvador

BRainE: So? I see that u r back from the movies. How did it go?

BigSl: What? U mean it didn't make the evening news?

BRainE: Okay, so not 2 good?

BigSl: No way. Elizabeth and Jessica made a big scene in front of the theater. They just about scratched each other's eyes out. Or at least they acted like they wanted to.

BRainE: Oh no! You mean they didn't make up?

BigSl: Not even close.

BRainE: Bummer. So much 4 plan A.

BigSl: Tell me about it. So what's plan B?

BRainE: I'm all out of ideas. Did u talk to Damon and Blue about it?

BigSl: Not really. We got separated at the theater. I sat with Anna and her drama pals. It was nice to get away from the whole Wakefield mess.

BRainE: I hear you. Kristin and I went out 4 pizza 2 night. She sez J is acting so psycho, it's scary. :-o

BigSl: Both twins are way over the cuckoo's nest by now.

BRainE: Yikes.

BigSl: U got that right.

A n n a

For some reason, out of the entire evening at the movies, there were these two specific images I couldn't get out of my head. The first one was how Larissa looked when we were hanging out with Toby in line—the happy expression on her face, the comfortable way her hand rested on his shoulder for just a second. The other image was Larissa's face when she'd returned to find me and Toby joking around without her. Her smile had sort of crumpled a little at the corners, like she was pretending it didn't bother her. But I could tell it did.

I've got to be the worst friend in the history of the world, I thought as I pulled down the comforter on my bed. Elizabeth was in the bathroom, brushing her teeth, which gave me a few minutes to myself to think. *Larissa trusted me—she told me how she feels about Toby. And what do I do? I fall for him myself.*

I grimaced at the thought. What was wrong

with me? Hadn't I learned a thing from the Elizabeth-Salvador-me fiasco?

Just then Elizabeth let herself into my room, already dressed in her pajamas. She'd been pretty quiet ever since we got home from the movies half an hour or so earlier. For once she wasn't babbling on and on about how Jessica had done her wrong. I wondered if that meant anything.

"Whew!" I said, trying to sound normal. "I'm beat. Ready to hit the sack?"

"Sure." Elizabeth glanced at her watch as she took it off her wrist. It was only about ten-fifteen, but she didn't mention that. Neither did I. So much for those all-night talk fests I'd imagined. "I just want to brush my hair first, okay?"

I nodded and slid into bed, pulling the covers up over my stomach. Was this new, quiet mood a sign that Elizabeth was finally ready to stop obsessing and start acting like a normal friend again? I hoped so. I missed the old Elizabeth— the one who was always ready to listen, to sympathize and give advice. I could use a friend like that at the moment. Big time.

"So, did you have a good time tonight?" I asked tentatively. Suddenly realizing what a stupid question that was, I laughed sheepishly. "I mean, aside from—you know."

Elizabeth shrugged. She sat down cross-legged on her sleeping bag, which was set up at the foot of my bed. Grabbing a brush out of her open suitcase nearby, she started brushing her long, blond hair. "It was okay, I guess."

"Yeah. For me too." I hesitated, wondering how to bring up the topic that was filling my mind. Elizabeth still seemed a little distracted. Was there even any point in trying to get her to focus on anyone but her twin?

Before I could decide, the door opened slightly.

"Anna?" My mom stuck her head into the room.

I winced. Half of Mom's black hair was braided, and the other half was hanging loose. Besides that, she was wearing her old pink bathrobe. That was a bad sign.

"Um, hi, Mom," I said cautiously. She'd been in the shower when Elizabeth and I got home from the movies, so this was the first time I'd seen her since dinnertime. "What's up?"

"I was just checking," Mom said vaguely.

Checking what? I wondered. But I knew better than to ask. I shot a quick glance at Elizabeth, who was staring down at her sleeping bag. "Okay, Mom," I said. "Um, good night."

"Good night, dear." Mom smiled, though her eyes didn't quite seem to be focused on me. And she had apparently forgotten that Elizabeth was there at all since she didn't so much as glance in her direction.

I sighed as she slipped out of the doorway and disappeared. Ever since my older brother, Tim, died in a car accident a little over a year ago, Mom has really had a tough time of it. We all have, actually. But either it hit her even harder than the rest of the family, or she was a lot worse at hiding it. Because up until just a few weeks ago, she spent most of her time in that bathrobe, wandering around the house like some kind of living ghost.

The rustle of nylon nearby snapped me out of my thoughts. Looking over, I saw that Elizabeth was sliding into her sleeping bag. "Good night," she said quietly when she caught my gaze.

"Good night." I was a little embarrassed, even though Elizabeth already knew all about my family's problems. I hate it when Mom slips back into one of her pink-bathrobe moods. Somehow it seems even harder to deal with now that she's finally started getting better. She's had more good days than bad lately, so I guess that makes the bad ones really stand out.

Elizabeth turned over on her side, facing away from me. I reached over to flip off the light switch. It was time to fall asleep and forget all about this whole depressing day.

Jessica Wakefield's Thrilling Sunday Afternoon

1:15 P.M.   Jessica finishes lunch and goes into the den. Her mom comes in and tells her to make the "bed."

"Why should I bother?" Jessica mutters, flopping down on top of her sheets as her mother hurries out of the room. "It's not like anyone is going to see it except me."

2:35 P.M.   After determining that there's nothing on TV except golf and some professional-bowling championship, Jessica turns off the set and wanders into the kitchen to get a soda. She calls Kristin to see if she wants to go to the mall, but she's not home. Then she calls Bethel to see if she wants to go for a run. But she's not home either. She considers calling Damon but decides she's still mad at him. Jessica wanders back into the den, deciding professional bowling isn't so boring after all. At least not compared to staring at the wall. Or doing algebra homework.

3:09 P.M.   Mr. Wakefield comes into the den, looking for a place to read his newspaper.

Seeing the messy sofa, he tells Jessica to straighten up the room. After he leaves, Jessica glances around. "Who cares if it's a mess in here?" she says out loud. "It fits my mood. I am one with my surroundings." Flopping back on the sofa cushions, she focuses again on the bowler on the TV screen.

3:42 P.M. The phone rings. Hoping it's Kristin or Bethel calling her back, Jessica leaps for it. But it's just some high-school girl calling for Steven. She sighs. Once again she realizes her loser older brother has a better social life than she does. And that's *truly* pathetic. Deciding she's not going to let her fight with Elizabeth ruin her life, she gets up and heads for the door. The least she can do is go for a run by herself to stay in shape.

3:59 P.M. Jessica is back on the couch again. It's too hot out to run, and besides, she just doesn't have the energy. And professional bowling is kind of interesting when you get into it. Really.

4:47 P.M. Mrs. Wakefield comes in to ask Jessica what she wants for dinner. When she sees the room, she frowns.

Why hasn't Jessica cleaned up yet? Jessica shushes her. "Just give me a second, Mom," she says urgently. "The last bowler is about to take his last shot, and I really want to see how it all turns out."

4:48 P.M. Realizing what she just said, Jessica gasps with terror. Things are even worse than she thought. She's actually getting totally involved in watching . . . bowling! Horrified, she quickly switches off the TV and starts cleaning up the room. Her mother is amazed.

5:20 P.M. The den is spotless, and dinner won't be ready for another hour. Jessica sits down and switches on the TV again. The bowling championship is over, and the only thing she can find to watch is a special on transplanting shrubs.

"Oh, well," she murmurs, settling back on the couch. "At least it's not golf."

Blue

"You should have seen her face when she ran off. She was, like, steaming mad," I said, wrapping some melted cheese around one finger. I popped it in my mouth and glanced across the table at Damon and Salvador. It was Sunday afternoon, and the three of us were hanging at Vito's, chowing down on pizza and talking about the Wakefield twins. I didn't know about anyone else, but the spinach-and-extra-cheese special was helping me feel better. At least a little.

Damon sighed. "I know exactly what you mean," he said. "Jessica looked like she was ready to strangle me when she thought I was taking her sister's side." He poked at his own slice, looking depressed.

I knew how he felt. Just when I thought I was really connecting with Elizabeth, I'd blown it. And I wasn't even sure how.

"I guess maybe we shouldn't have gotten

in their business," I said. "They just have to work things out for themselves."

"Maybe," Damon agreed uncertainly. "Anyway, our plan definitely bombed big time."

Salvador waved one hand expressively. Swallowing a huge mouthful of pizza, he shook his head. "So plan A tanked," he said. "So what? There's always plan B."

"There is?" Damon asked. "Okay, what is it?"

Salvador rolled his eyes. "Well, I don't know right this second," he said. "I mean, I don't have anything specific worked out yet. But I'm sure we can come up with something."

I wasn't so sure about that myself. Still, Salvador had been friends with Elizabeth longer than I had. Maybe he knew what he was talking about.

"Okay, then," I said. "We know the twins are mad at each other. We know they're both acting kind of, um . . ."

"Unreasonable?" Damon suggested.

"Obnoxious?" Salvador put in.

"Irrational?" Damon added.

"Psychotic?" Salvador said.

"Let me guess," a new voice broke in. "You're talking about Elizabeth and Jessica."

Glancing up, I saw that Anna had just

118

reached our table. I gulped, looking over her shoulder.

"Don't worry, Elizabeth isn't with me," Anna said, seeing what I was doing. "She's at my house, doing homework. I needed a break, so I told her I had to run out and buy shampoo. But I saw you guys in the window, so I figured I'd better stop in and make sure you're still coming to the *Zone* meeting tonight, Salvador." She stared pointedly at him. Sal has been part of the online 'zine since it started. I'd thought about going to meetings, mostly as a way to hang out more with Elizabeth. Of course, hanging out with Elizabeth didn't sound quite as fun at the moment as it usually did.

"Tonight?" Salvador repeated. "Oh yeah. I almost forgot about that." He didn't look too thrilled.

Damon shrugged. "Hey, at least you'll only have one twin to deal with."

"Watch out, or we may draft you," Salvador joked. "Besides, Elizabeth's harder to deal with than Jessica. You got the easy twin."

"Get real!" Damon shook his head. "Elizabeth is a piece of cake."

"Oh yeah?" Anna said. "You're only saying that because you don't have to live with her.

Blue

Hearing about how awful Jessica is all day every day isn't easy, you know."

Salvador puffed out his chest. "True," he said. "Then again, I'm the only one here who's tried to talk to both of them. That's real courage."

Anna rolled her eyes. "Please," she told me, shaking her head. "Real courage is sleeping in the same room with Elizabeth. I'm lucky she doesn't sleepwalk over and murder me, thinking I'm Jessica."

"Well, I was lucky to get away from Jessica yesterday without getting punched in the face," Damon put in. "I'm telling you, Anna, you're not the only one scared for your life."

"Maybe we should change our song. Instead of 'I Wanna Be Your Twin' it could be 'I Wanna Flee the Twins,'" Salvador joked.

I smiled grimly. They were all getting a little carried away, but it was no wonder. The twins' feud was putting us all on edge. "Okay, enough," I said. "We all know they're both toxically annoying these days, but Sal was right earlier."

"I was?" Salvador looked surprised. "Um, about what?"

"We need a plan B," I replied. "We have to figure out how to end this stupid fight ASAP so things can get back to normal."

Damon and Salvador looked uncertain. But Anna's eyes lit up.

"I just thought of a plan," she said, looking hopeful and a little cautious. "I'm not sure if it's really stupid or not."

"Well, any plan's better than no plan," Salvador said. "So let's hear it."

There was a full house at the *Zone* meeting on Sunday night. We met at Brian Rainey's place. Brian had missed out on the fun the night before, but he couldn't possibly miss the tension in the room when we all sat down in front of his computer.

Meanwhile I was feeling a little queasy. Plan B, as we were calling it, depended a lot on me. It was more pressure than I liked—I was nervous about screwing up and making things worse. But Anna had insisted that I was the only one who could pull it off without making either Elizabeth or Jessica suspicious, and Salvador and Damon agreed with her, so I was outvoted. I mean, I had been getting more involved in after-school activities lately, so I knew it wouldn't look too weird for me to be here. But still—democracy stinks sometimes.

It was a relief when Elizabeth called the

meeting to order. "First of all, glad to have you on the team, Blue." She smiled at me. *So far, so good,* I thought. "Now. We should concentrate on content tonight. We never really covered it the other day, and we need to start putting some new stuff out there. Different, interesting articles and features. We want people to keep coming back to our site over and over again."

Brian nodded. "We should have some variety," he said. "I think we need more movie and music reviews. Those have been really popular so far. Does anyone want to write something about *The Getaway,* like Anna suggested at the last meeting? You all saw it last night, right?"

There was dead silence. Sure, we'd seen it—technically. I know I barely remembered the plot, and at least I'd been in the theater the whole time—unlike some people. But after Elizabeth ran out, I was so distracted that I might as well have been watching a test pattern on TV.

Finally Salvador spoke up. "I'll do it," he said. "I, uh, really paid attention during the movie."

Noticing Anna shooting me looks, I cleared my throat. "Dudes," I said. "I have an idea for a story."

"What is it?" Elizabeth asked, looking a little tense.

I shrugged, trying to sound natural. "Okay, like, I was watching this show on cable, and it was all about twins and what it's like, you know, psychologically, to be a twin. Really interesting stuff." I paused, hoping Elizabeth wouldn't remember I'd rather surf than watch TV. "And you know how when there's a special like that on TV, it catches on? Like one show does a special on animals going berserk, and all of a sudden every other network does a show on it, and people just eat it up? Anyway, it's a good way to stir up buzz. I thought maybe I could do a story on you—like, what it's really all about being a twin, stuff like that. You know, Sweet Valley's own twin story."

Elizabeth's face had darkened when I first said the word *twins*. She frowned at me. "I don't think so," she said stiffly. "It doesn't really seem like news to me."

"Hey, don't worry," I said. I was prepared for that exact response. "I know you're steamed at Jessica right now. But you won't have to talk about her at all, I swear. Just answer a few questions, you know, like an interview or whatever. No big."

"It sounds cool," Brian said. Anna and Sal nodded encouragingly.

Elizabeth shrugged, looking as reluctant as ever. Even a little suspicious, which wasn't surprising after our conversation last night. I took a deep breath.

"Come on, it'll be fun," I added, still trying to sound casual. "And interesting for our audience too. It's a human-interest story, isn't it? Anyway, you really shouldn't put a tiff with your sister above the good of the 'zine."

I held my breath, waiting for her reaction. That last comment wasn't like me at all, but Anna had assured me that it would be the perfect way to guilt Elizabeth into agreeing. Either that or it would make her hate me forever. At least that was what I was afraid of.

Elizabeth was still frowning. But finally she nodded. "Okay," she said slowly. "But I'll only do it if I definitely *don't* have to deal with Jessica. If that's what you guys want to get out of this, by any chance, it's *not* going to happen."

"Deal," I said, letting out a silent sigh of relief. Apparently Anna had been right. "I won't even mention her name."

"Okay." Elizabeth shrugged. "Jessica never

reads *Zone* anyway. So I guess it'll be all right."

"Cool." As soon as Elizabeth turned away to say something to Brian, I gave Anna and Salvador a relieved grin. Plan B was well under way.

Jessica

". . . Anyway, I'm glad we talked." Damon was giving me that amazing smile of his, the one that makes my toes quiver.

"Me too," I said softly, leaning against my locker. I really did feel bad about taking out my problems with the amazing two-faced queen of selfishness—also known as my sister—on him. "And I'm sorry again for yelling at you the other night."

"No problem." Damon reached for my hand, making my skin tingle. "I'm just glad we're okay now."

"Me too," I repeated. Now I was wishing I'd called him the day before, especially since I'd spent the entire day watching lame stuff on TV and breathing in the paint fumes that drifted down from upstairs. It would serve Elizabeth right if I ended up with some kind of weird paint-poisoning disease from being stuck in the house all weekend. Maybe then she would remember that I existed. She might even wish she'd spent more time with me when she had the chance. But it would be too late. Ha!

I was thinking about that when I noticed Elizabeth's friend Blue wandering toward us. To my surprise, he walked right up to us, a goofy, spacey sort of smile on his face.

"Uh, hello?" I said. "Can we help you?"

"Hey, guys," he replied. "How's it going?"

I sighed. Why did Elizabeth's friends have to start bugging me now? First Salvador dropped by the house to chat the other day, and now Blue suddenly decided he wanted to hang with me at school.

Damon didn't seem to notice how strange it was, though. I guess he thought it was normal since they're in that band together. "Everything's cool," he said to Blue. "How are things with you?"

"I'm getting by." Blue blinked at me, still with that same lazy smile. "So, Jessica—I was wondering if I could interview you for this piece I'm writing."

"Interview me?" Suddenly I was a whole lot more interested in what he was saying. I love being interviewed. Just a few weeks earlier a reporter from the local Sweet Valley newspaper came to one of our track meets. She asked me a few questions afterward and then ended up using my name in her article. It was really cool. I cut out the article and saved it. "Wait a minute," I added, a little suspicious. As far as I knew, the Sweet Valley paper wasn't hiring eighth-graders to write personality profiles. "What kind of piece? Who are you writing it for?"

"It's about twins. It's based on this special I saw on TV the other night. And it's for, you know, *Zone*," Blue mumbled, looking kind of sheepish.

"I knew it!" I exclaimed. I couldn't believe he expected me to contribute to Elizabeth's stupid little online 'zine. "Forget it. I'm not interested in being interviewed for *Zone*." I folded my arms over my chest to emphasize my point.

Blue cocked his head. "Are you sure?" he asked. "I mean, I respect your choice and all. But I really think you should consider this. It won't take long, and I promise you don't have to talk about Elizabeth at all if you don't want to."

I rolled my eyes. "She's my twin," I reminded him. "If I don't talk about her, what's to talk about?"

"Yourself," Blue replied promptly. "I'm more interested in what being a twin is really like for *you*. Your personal experience, you know?"

I hesitated. That didn't sound too bad. In fact, it sounded kind of interesting. But still, I wasn't thrilled about the idea of appearing in *Zone*, which probably should have been named *Zoned Out*. Most of the articles were pretty boring. At least they were the one time I'd checked it out. "I don't know . . . ," I said dubiously.

Damon nudged me in the side. "Hey, come on, Jessica," he said teasingly. "I was already looking forward to having a famous girlfriend."

I glanced over at him quickly. "Really?" I asked, suddenly feeling a little shy. Damon and I had a few problems when we first started going steady. We were so busy trying to live up to being the perfect boyfriend and girlfriend that we sort of forgot why we got together in the first place. We worked things out eventually, but ever since then we hadn't really referred to each other as boyfriend and girlfriend, at least not when we were talking to each other. It was kind of nice to realize that Damon still thought of me as his girlfriend.

"Yeah," he said with a smile. "You'd practically be a celebrity, you know? At least to me." He blushed slightly and glanced down at his hands. "Anyway," he added, "what's the big deal? So Blue asks you a few questions. It could be fun."

"Right," Blue put in. "You don't have to answer anything you don't want to. Total low-pressure interview."

I chewed my lower lip for a second, looking from one guy to the other. Damon was right. It wasn't a big deal. Besides, why should my stupid problems with Elizabeth make me miss out on seeing my name in print? Even if it was only on her lame Web page.

Finally I smiled. "Okay," I told Blue. "I'll do it. But only if I don't have to talk about Elizabeth at all."

Identical Twins—An Investigative Report, by Blue Spiccoli
Interview with E. Wakefield

Q. *What does being a twin mean to you?*

A. It's just a biological term, really. I mean, it's not like it defines my whole life or anything. No way. Other people make a bigger deal out of it than they should, if you ask me.

Q. *When did you first realize that being a twin makes you different?*

A. It doesn't make me different. Except that other people think it does. I guess I first realized that pretty young, like probably the first time my twin and I switched places and fooled everyone. Most people can't do that, I guess.

Q. *How does being a twin make you feel different from most people?*

A. Well, I suppose if it makes me feel different at all, it's because I know I'll never be alone. There will always be someone who knows me really well out there. Of course, that can be a good thing or a bad thing, depending.

Q. *What is the hardest thing about being a twin?*

A. Everyone always expects us to be exactly alike, just because we look the same on the outside. And we're not. It can be really frustrating sometimes—like you have to fight to make people see you as an individual and not part of a matched set. To realize that you have your own totally unique personality, just like everyone else. I think maybe that's something only another identical twin can understand.

Q. *Do you ever wish you weren't a twin?*

A. Um . . . I've never really thought about it like that. I'd have to say no. We have our differences, but Jessica and I have had lots of fun together over the years. You wouldn't think so since we don't have that much in common. But that doesn't mean I don't like hanging out with her and being her twin.

Q. *What is the coolest thing about being a twin?*

A. I guess when it comes right down to it, having a twin is special. Jessica drives me nuts a lot of the time, but deep down, I know she's my best friend. She's the one person who means the most to me in the world. And that's never going to change.

Identical Twins—An Investigative Report, by Blue Spiccoli Interview with J. Wakefield

Q. What does being a twin mean to you?

A. It means always having someone my exact size trying to borrow all my clothes.

Q. When did you first realize that being a twin makes you different?

A. I don't know. Boring question. Next?

Q. How does being a twin make you feel different from most people?

A. Most people don't have twins. Duh. Come on, Blue, do your questions get any better than this?

Q. What is the hardest thing about being a twin?

A. Okay, that's more like it. Being a twin is tougher than it looks. There's the clothes thing, like I already mentioned. And another thing, you always have to deal with people mixing you up, which is superannoying. Well, unless you're trying to fool them, of course. Then it's kind of cool having someone who looks exactly like you.

Q. Do you ever wish you weren't a twin?

A. Um . . . no, I guess not. I mean, I can't imagine not having Liz around. We do hang out a lot. You know. Just talking and stuff. And sometimes there are things that only a twin can really understand, so it's handy having one around. I guess I'm sort of lucky if you look at it like that. Of course, it's hard sometimes because other people can really, uh . . . What was the question again?

Q. *What is the coolest thing about being a twin?*
   A. Well, we may not be getting along that great lately, and she may be really annoying sometimes. But . . . Okay, I know I can count on her when it's really important. It's weird. Elizabeth is like the other half of me or something. And I guess most of the time, that's pretty cool.

Jessica

"There you are!" I exclaimed, spotting Damon hunched over a monitor in the school's computer lab the next afternoon. "I've been looking all over the building for you since track practice let out. What are you doing?"

Damon glanced up and blinked at me. "Oh! Sorry, Jessica," he said, checking his watch. "I guess I lost track of the time."

I almost made a comment about how this was the second time he'd left me hanging in three days, but I bit my tongue. I didn't want to bring up that whole tired subject again. The only reason he didn't show when he was supposed to on Saturday was because of Salvador's pathetic plan to force me to make up with Elizabeth. I blamed Salvador, not him. Actually, the person I really blamed was Elizabeth herself. But like I said, I didn't want to think about that.

Doing my best to forget all about my twin, I walked over and perched on the desk beside Damon. "Okay, no big." I smiled at him. "Ready to hit the mall? I've been dying for a strawberry milk shake since fifth period. So let's motor!"

"In a second." Damon hit a few keys on the keyboard. "I was just going to check out the new issue of *Zone*. Salvador told me it just went up today."

I raised an eyebrow at him. "*Zone*?" I repeated. "Since when do you read *Zone*?"

"Since they decided to interview you, remember?" He smiled. "Jessica Wakefield, world-famous twin? I just wanted to see how it turned out."

"Oh!" I'd almost forgotten about that. The interview with Blue had been really short and pretty lame. Plus I'd ended up dredging up all sorts of stuff from the past, which I really hoped he didn't use. It was mostly pretty dorky. "Um, I'm sure it's stupid," I told Damon nervously, not sure I wanted him to see it. I also wasn't sure that *I* wanted to see it. "Come on, why waste your time? It's, like, thirty seconds you'll never get back again."

He grinned at me. "Feeling shy?" he teased.

I grimaced. Still, I couldn't help being curious. I leaned over Damon's shoulder as he clicked on the welcome icon on the 'zine's home page. To my surprise, the page actually looked kind of cool—lots of color, fun icons, the works. I guessed Brian Rainey had something to do with that. It certainly didn't look like the kind of thing the others would come up with in a million years.

"Hurry up," I muttered anxiously. "Let's get this over with so we can eat."

As the page loaded, I stepped back a little. I still wasn't sure I wanted to see it. But Damon leaned forward to read. "Hey," he said after a second. "Did you know they interviewed Elizabeth too?"

"What?" I peered over his shoulder again. "I can't believe it! He said there wouldn't be anything about her in this article."

Damon cleared his throat. "Actually, I think what he said was that you wouldn't have to talk about Elizabeth," he corrected. "Not that he wouldn't include her at all."

I frowned. "Whatever," I said. "I still can't believe that he did this. It's totally deceitful."

Damon didn't answer. I leaned forward to read more. It looked like Blue had asked Elizabeth the exact same questions he asked me. I scowled as I read her first response. She babbled on and on about how being a twin didn't mean anything to her at all.

"Nice," I muttered sarcastically. "Just when I thought she was as rude as she could be, she goes and gets ruder. Did you check out her first answer?" I poked Damon on the shoulder. "Now do you see why I'm so mad at her?"

Damon gestured at the screen. "Um, maybe you should keep reading," he suggested. "It gets more interesting."

I rolled my eyes. Nothing my twin had to say seemed very interesting to me. But I read on. The next few answers were pretty much what I would have expected. But then I reached the last couple of responses.

"Am I imagining things?" I murmured, reading the last one again. "Or did she actually say some really nice things about me?"

"You're not imagining things," Damon replied.

I glanced at him, realizing I'd almost forgotten he was there. Suddenly I didn't feel much like going to the mall anymore. Reading what Elizabeth had said was making me feel kind of sad. Would we ever be that close again?

"Look, can I take a rain check on that milk shake?" I asked Damon. "I'm actually not in the mood anymore."

Elizabetn

I tapped my fingers impatiently on Anna's desk while I waited for her computer to boot up. "I hope all the new design stuff is working right. Brian uploaded everything during his study hall today, but I haven't had a chance to look at it until now."

"Me either," Anna replied from across the room, where she was dumping her textbooks out of her backpack onto a big pile on her bed.

Finally the computer was ready, and I pulled up the *Zone* home page. "Wow," I said. "The home page looks great!" Even though I'd seen most of it at the meeting, I was still way impressed. Brian had really done a fantastic job of jazzing up our site. I quickly scanned the table of contents, checking to make sure all the new stories were there.

Anna wandered over to look over my shoulder. "Hey, I almost forgot," she said, pointing at an entry near the bottom of the list. "Blue's twin story. Have you checked it out yet?"

Elizabeth

"No," I replied. I'd managed to mostly put that interview out of my mind. Afterward I sort of wished that Blue hadn't talked me into doing it. I ended up saying some stuff that was sort of private. "Salvador edited that one."

"Well?" Anna said expectantly. "Aren't you going to read it now?"

I bit my lip. There didn't seem to be much I could do about the interview now except hope that it didn't make me sound too lame. "Sure, I guess," I said shortly.

Moving the mouse, I clicked on the icon. The page loaded quickly. When I saw the headline, I blinked.

"Hey, wait a minute," I said. "It looks like he interviewed Jessica too!"

"Looks that way," Anna agreed.

I glanced over my shoulder at her, suddenly suspicious. She didn't sound very surprised to learn that Blue had sneaked my twin into his story. Still, I supposed it made sense. Why write a story about twins without mentioning both of us? "I guess he never really said he wouldn't mention her," I murmured with a twinge of annoyance. Who knew Blue could be so sneaky? "He just said he wouldn't make *me* talk about her."

Anna didn't reply. She was looking at the

screen, her dark eyes flitting back and forth as she read the interviews.

I started to read too. As soon as I scanned Jessica's first answer, I snorted. "Typical," I muttered. "She's still harping on that stupid shirt. Anyway, she's the one who's always borrowing my clothes, not the other way around. Half the time she never bothers to return them either. I have to go in and dig them out from the back of her closet or under her bed. Once I even found my favorite pair of cargo shorts stuffed way down in the bottom of her stinky old gym bag, and it took me three washes to—"

"Elizabeth!" Anna interrupted. "Did you read the rest of her answers?"

"I don't need to," I replied with a frown. "I know what they're going to say. Jessica is totally predictable."

Anna shrugged and pointed at the screen. "I don't know," she said. "But I never would have expected her to say some of this stuff about you. Especially now."

"What kind of stuff?" I mumbled, mostly to myself. Glancing at the screen again, I quickly read the next couple of responses. No surprises there.

Then I got to the question about the best thing we'd done together as twins. When I scanned Jessica's answer, I thought for a second that I'd read it wrong. I went back and read it again more slowly.

"Wow," I said, swallowing hard. "It almost sort of sounds like she, you know, *misses* me or something. Anyway, I didn't know she still felt that way—lucky to have me around."

"Did you see the last one?" Anna asked softly.

I quickly read that response too. All of a sudden I felt completely horrible, like the most selfish and petty person in the world. How could I have been so stupid? What were Jessica and I fighting about anyway?

I sat back in my chair, staring blankly at the computer screen. All of a sudden a wave of homesickness washed over me. Or maybe it was *twin* sickness. Either way, I knew I had to get out of there.

"Anna?" I said. "Um, don't take this the wrong way, but I have to go home. Now."

Jessica

I was making myself some nachos in the microwave when I heard the back door open. Glancing over, I saw Elizabeth coming in with her suitcase.

I stared at her in surprise. When I first got home a little while earlier, I'd sort of hoped she might be there. After reading her answers in *Zone,* I thought maybe she would want to talk or something. But when I got home to an empty house—well, Steven was there, and the painters, but that hardly counts—I figured maybe I was reading too much into it.

Now I wasn't sure what to think. So I just kept watching her as she walked into the kitchen and put her suitcase on the floor near the table. She saw me looking at her and met my eyes.

"Hi," she said softly.

I cleared my throat. "Hey." Just then the microwave beeped. My nachos were done.

Turning away from my twin, I popped open

the microwave and grabbed the plate. I set it on the counter and blew on the melted cheese to cool it off a little.

Then I glanced at Elizabeth again. She was still standing there, watching me. "So anyway," I said, "I was just watching *Pool Party II*. Dad rented it for me last night, but I didn't get around to watching it then. Want to watch with me now? It just started—I could rewind it if you want."

"Sure," Elizabeth said, smiling a little. "That would be really great."

I started to breathe a little easier. Did this mean she was as sick of fighting as I was? Picking up my nachos, I led the way into the den. My pillows and sheets and stuff were all over the place, but I shoved them onto the floor so Elizabeth would have a place to sit.

"Thanks," she said, leaning back against the cushions. "Um, can I have a nacho?"

"Help yourself." I pushed the plate toward her, then grabbed the remote and hit the rewind button.

As the tape whirred backward, I glanced at my sister. She was wiping a spot of melted cheese off her lip.

She saw me looking at her and smiled sheepishly. "This is nice," she said. "It's been a while since the two of us watched a movie together."

"I know." I hesitated, sort of afraid to go on. But I knew I had to tell her how I was feeling. It was the only way we would ever really make up—and I was tired of feeling so bad. I took a deep breath. "Um, I kind of wish we could do more stuff like this. Together."

"Really?" Elizabeth turned to face me. "I've been thinking the same thing."

"You have?" I was a little surprised. "It hasn't really seemed that way lately. You know, with the way you rushed off to stay with Anna instead of . . ."

I let my voice trail off. I knew I sounded really needy and, well, kind of pathetic. I guess spending the week feeling like I had no friends hadn't exactly boosted my self-confidence.

Elizabeth gasped. "Is that why you've been acting so—um, seemed so upset this past week?" she asked. "Because I went to stay at Anna's instead of staying here with you?"

I had been waiting for days now for Elizabeth to clue in to what I was angry about. I thought once she figured out why I was mad, she'd admit that she was wrong and that I'd feel much better. But things weren't going the way I'd planned. Suddenly the situation didn't seem so black-and-white anymore.

Jessica

And there was something else. Now that we were finally talking, I realized I didn't feel mad anymore. I just felt kind of sad.

I shrugged. "I guess," I admitted. "I mean, it wasn't the fact that you went to Anna's. It was just, well, I was thinking it would be so much fun to camp out here in the den." I waved a hand at the messy room. "Just the two of us, like when we used to share a room when we were younger. And then you just ran off to your friend's house like you never even thought about it."

"You've got it all wrong!" she exclaimed, looking upset. "Of course I thought about it. It was the first thing that popped into my head. But I thought you'd be glad to have the space." She tucked her legs under her. "You've always been the social one, Jess. I mean, between Damon, your new friends, and the track team, you've got a new social world here. My life may not seem all that exciting to you, but I like my new friends, and I'm having fun." She sighed. "Anyway, I thought things were going along as always—you doing your thing, me doing mine. So I just figured it would be kind of a minivacation for both of us if I wasn't around." She looked down. "Plus I didn't think you'd want to sleep in the den with me."

"Why wouldn't I?" I asked in surprise.

She shrugged. "I don't know," she said softly. "I guess I was just worried that you might think it was silly to want to hang out together for a whole week. Or that you might get bored."

I felt a twinge of guilt, remembering how I'd called Anna boring.

Staring at me earnestly, Elizabeth bit her lip. "The truth is, there's nobody I'd rather hang out with than you, Jess. Not Anna, not anyone."

"Really?" I smiled. Suddenly it seemed as if a huge weight had been lifted from my shoulders. I realized that was all I needed to hear. "Same goes for me," I told her shyly.

I thought about what Elizabeth was saying. It was true, back at our old school I'd always had lots of friends to do fun stuff with. Elizabeth had always had just a few, very close friends and liked to do quieter things with them like write and study. That's the way it had always been between us, and it never bothered me before.

But now it seemed like something was kind of switched. Now Elizabeth was the one who was out doing things with her friends, like hanging out at Blue's house, playing volleyball, or meeting Anna and Sal for *Zone* meetings and movies. Sure, I had friends and wasn't usually moping around the house like a social reject, but I had to admit that since we started at SVJH, things had been a little quiet for me. And I guess it was bumming me out more than I'd thought.

I looked into my twin's eyes. "I'm sorry I was so harsh about your friends," I said. "Look, the important thing is for us to not take each other for granted, right?"

"Right," Elizabeth agreed. "And we should make sure we always tell each other how we're feeling."

I smiled back at her. It felt good to be connecting again. It felt like it had been a while since we really saw things the same way.

Suddenly Elizabeth cringed.

"What's wrong?" I asked.

"I was just thinking—we haven't exactly been fun to be around this week. Our friends must be so mad at us!"

I bit my lip. "I know, you're right. I mean, I've talked it out with Damon, but . . ." I thought about how I'd barely spoken to Kristin or Bethel and when I had, I'd been a major pain. "We've got some major apologizing ahead of us."

At that moment Steven hurried into the room, sniffing like a bloodhound on a scent. "Do I smell nachos?" he asked.

"Get your own!" I told him, shielding the

plate as he made a beeline for it. "These are for Liz and me."

He stopped short, blinking at the two of us in surprise. "Wait a minute," he said. "What's wrong with this picture? I thought you two were, like, mortal enemies now."

"Go away, Steven," I told him. But I couldn't hide my smile. I was so relieved that Elizabeth and I weren't mad at each other anymore, even Steven couldn't spoil my good mood.

He grinned. "*Awww.* Did you two finally kiss and make up? Go on! Kiss and make up!" He came over and shoved us toward each other, making kissy noises.

I was annoyed at his corny, stupid behavior. But when I felt Elizabeth's arm slip around my shoulders, I couldn't help reaching out and hugging her back.

"I'm glad we're friends again," she whispered in my ear, too quietly for Steven to overhear.

I squeezed her tightly, ignoring the fact that our brother was gobbling down our nachos. "*Best* friends," I whispered back.

Check out the **all-new**....

.... (Sweet Valley Web site—

www.sweetvalley.com

New Features

Cool Prizes

The ONLY official Web site!

Hot Links

(And much more!)

SWEET VALLEY

Francine Pascal's

jr. high

You hate your **alarm clock.**

You hate your **clothes.**

You're going
to love
Jr. High.

Bantam

www.sweetvalley.com